SNEAK ATTACK!

THE GRUBSTAKE ADVENTURES

SNEAK ATTACK!

NATHAN AASENG

Augsburg
MINNEAPOLIS

SNEAK ATTACK!

Cover art and design by Dawn Mathers

Library of Congress Cataloging-in-Publication Data

Aaseng, Nathan
    Sneak Attack! / Nathan Aaseng.
      p. cm.— (The Grubstake Adventures)
      Summary: Tanya learns important lessons in trust and forgiveness when the girls' retaliation for a prank played by some boys at Camp Grubstake escalates the teasing to a dangerous level.
      ISBN 0-8066-2787-5 (pbk.)
      [1. Camps—Fiction. 2. Revenge—Fiction. 3. Bedwetting—Fiction.
    4. Christian life—Fiction.] I. Title. II. Series.
    PZ7.A13Sn   1995
    [Fic]—dc20   94-44807
                                                                              CIP
                                                                              AC

The paper used in this publication meets the minimum requirements of American National Standard for Information Services—Permanence of Paper for Printed Library Materials, ANSI Z329.48-1984. ∞

Manufactured in the U.S.A.   AF 9-2787

99   98   97   96   95   1   2   3   4   5   6   7   8   9   10

CONTENTS

To the memory of Sparky Reynolds

ONE

Ambush

Is this place really safe?" Tanya asked as she waved the beam of her flashlight among the trees.

The farthest she had ever traveled from her pillow to a bathroom was up the stairs and down the hall. But now she and two friends were walking along the wagon trail to the only modern bathroom in Camp Horizon. Or "Camp Grubstake," as all the experienced campers called it. Dense forest and blackberry brambles pressed against the trail on all sides. Tanya shivered as she imagined beady eyes peering at her. She skittered away from branches that overhung the trail, fearful that some snake might be waiting to jump on her.

"Relax," said Allison, who had been to Grubstake the year before. "There's nothing dangerous around here. The bathroom is just around the corner."

But the corner was still beyond the reach of Tanya's flashlight beam. Darkness, deeper and wider than Tanya had ever known, closed in on all sides. Her puny flashlight seemed like a toy.

"Didn't someone say there were snakes in this valley?" she gulped.

"Stop being such a baby!" Courtney scolded. Unlike Tanya, she had gotten used to this camp immediately. "Was Poke here last year, Allison? I think she's cool."

"Yeah, we lucked out," Allison agreed. "She's the best counselor. She's nice, she's fun, and nobody can play a guitar like her."

Tanya shifted her towel and soap from one arm to the other. She tried to ignore her nerves. "What happens if it rains? That teepee we're in has a big hole in the middle. Don't you get soaked?"

"No," Allison said, patiently. "The rain runs down the teepee poles and—

"AIEEEEEEEE!"

Hideous shrieks ripped the darkness! The forest burst open with creatures crashing through branches! Allison and Courtney screamed and clenched their fists. Tanya jumped backwards and fell over Allison. Her heart banged so hard against her chest she could feel her ribs bend.

A light shone in Tanya's eyes. She squinted and turned her head. When she recovered her senses, she saw a large group of boys hooting and grinning.

"Hi, there," said Brad, whom Tanya recognized from her church. "Just thought we'd stop by and say hello."

Tanya was shaking. There were about a dozen ambushers. About half of them were familiar. She wanted to call them every insulting name she could think of. But she knew her voice would give away how much they had scared her. She would not give them the satisfaction.

Courtney was no help, Tanya thought disgustedly. She loved any kind of attention from boys. All she could do now was giggle.

Allison was the only one who stood up to them. "Real cute! What's the matter, did the little boys get lost in the big forest? Need someone to help you find your way home?"

"Right, Allison," said Brad. He was still grinning and the braces on his teeth shone in the dim light. "Try to act like you didn't get the winkies scared out of you."

"Who wouldn't be scared, seeing your ugly faces pop out of the woods at night," shot back Tanya. Just as she feared, her voice trembled as she said it.

"You girls are sure slow. We'd almost given up waiting for you," said another of the boys.

"Good. I hope you waited a long time," said Allison. "I hope a thousand mosquitoes bit you while you sat in those bushes. I hope you've got even more ticks in your hair than dandruff." Tanya gloated privately as she saw some of the boys secretly run a few fingers through their hair.

"A few bug bites is a small price to pay for the look on your face," said Brad with a smile.

"What are you doing out here, anyway?" said Allison. "Does your counselor know where you are?"

Brad shined his flashlight on his watch. "Hey, we'd better run. Red Dog wanted us back by ten o'clock. We only have four minutes."

"So what's he going to do if we're late?" sneered Darin. Tanya knew Darin by sight but didn't know much about him. He was a greasy, sullen-looking boy. Skinny, too. Nobody paid much attention to him at church, except when he got in trouble. Which was often enough. He once got kicked out of Sunday School class.

"Who knows?" one boy shrugged. "That Red Dog is one weird dude."

"Well, good night," said Brad to the girls, smiling. "Hope you don't have any nightmares. See you tomorrow." The boys ran down one of the side paths leading off from the wagon trail, celebrating with war whoops.

Tanya watched them leave, still smoldering. Her elbow hurt from her fall. "Bradley Walker is a dork," she said as they continued toward the bathroom. "Those guys think they're so cool. I could have had a heart attack."

"I think Brad's cute," said Courtney. "I love his dimples."

"So marry him!" scoffed Tanya.

The idea didn't seem to turn her off. "How far away is their camp?" Courtney asked.

"They must be over in Meadow Village," Allison said. "That's clear beyond the Old Grubstake."

It was amazing what anger could do for courage. For the moment Tanya barely noticed the darkness. The woods seemed no more threatening than a wallpapered hall. "What is all this grubstake stuff?" she asked. "Camp Grubstake. The Old Grubstake. It sounds so grungy."

"Grubstake was the name of this little building where some miners made their headquarters a long time ago," explained Allison. "I guess they were lead miners or something. Anyway, the Old Grubstake is still there. That's where the camp stores equipment like canoes and horse stuff. When they turned this place into a camp they called it Camp Horizon. But people around here were so used to calling it the Grubstake that they keep calling it that. Almost everyone calls it Camp Grubstake now except the director."

"So how far away is the boys' camp?" asked Courtney. Tanya rolled her eyes. That girl had a one-track mind.

"I don't know. Half-mile, maybe," said Allison. "Far enough so we won't have to see much of them."

"Lucky for them," Tanya said, seeing Courtney's disappointment.

In the faint glow of the flashlight, Allison's smile looked almost wicked. "Ohhhh, it's not *all* that far. Not so far that someone couldn't get over there and cause a little disturbance. If someone wanted to do that kind of thing."

Revenge sounded sweet to Tanya. Her elbow hurt and a quick inspection with her flashlight revealed grass stains on her blue jeans. "I'd love to pay them back," she said as they rounded the corner and trotted down the steep hill to the bathrooms. "What do you have in mind?"

The bathroom was full at the moment. As they stood outside waiting for their turn, Allison thought for a moment. "Brad was the ringleader, right?"

Courtney nodded eagerly. She didn't care about revenge but was obviously excited about any activity that involved Brad.

"Maybe we could pay them a visit tonight?" Allison offered. Courtney readily agreed.

"Can you do that?" Tanya asked. "I mean, can you get away with that?"

"Probably," said Allison. "Poke is the heaviest sleeper in the camp."

"What do we do when we get there?" Courtney asked breathlessly.

Allison sighed. "That's the problem. What do we do—scare them when they're sleeping? What if they catch us? Just the three of us alone in their village."

"I'd rather do something where we wouldn't be found out," Tanya said.

"Yeah, maybe so," Allison agreed with a shrug.

Courtney slumped in disappointment. "Well, that ends that."

They stood in silence for a moment. Tanya looked up at a sky that seemed to have swelled to double its normal size. The stars were as thick as if someone had dumped a giant bag of sugar in the sky. Suddenly Allison began jumping up and down. "Ooh hoo hoo, I've got it! I've got it!" she squealed. "I know just how to get back at Brad Walker."

As she said it, the bathroom door opened and a large group of girls from another village piled out.

"Those guys must have got you," one of them laughed. "We saw them in the bushes on our way here. They said they were going to scare the pants off some girls from Forest Village."

"They have a sick sense of humor. They'll pay for that," Tanya said.

"Why, what are you going to do?" asked one of the girls.

Tanya and Courtney looked blankly at Allison. "You'll find out tomorrow," Allison said with her nasty smile as she filed past them into the bathroom.

"Why, what are you going to do?"

Allison turned back to face them. "I'll give you a hint. Keep an eye on the flagpole tomorrow."

Tanya and Courtney joined Allison at the sink. Checking the door to see that no one else was coming in, Tanya whispered, "What's the plan? I thought we weren't going to sneak out of our camp tonight."

"We aren't," said Allison, scrubbing her face. "We don't have to. "We're going to get Brad Walker in broad daylight!"

Horse Trail

R ed Dog picked up the first of Brad's pancakes with his fingertips and scowled. "Is this a pancake, or were you out collecting road kill this morning?" he asked.

"You're the one who's making me do this," Brad said. "What do you expect? I've never made pancakes before."

"Have you ever seen a pancake? I was hoping you'd have a rough idea of what they were supposed to look like," Red Dog said. He inspected the inch-thick mass. It was charred on the outside and oozed batter from the inside.

"That was my first try. You think you can do better, you make them," said Brad. Cooking had always been pure magic to him. Mom or Dad performed some tricks on the stove and presto! Cooked food magically appeared at the table. He didn't know how they did it. He certainly didn't know what he was doing now.

Red Dog smiled sweetly and patted Brad on the shoulder. He was a huge guy with wavy red hair. Curly red whiskers covered his cheeks. The red bandana he had tied over his hair made him look like a pirate. His large chest was covered with only a fringed, sleeveless vest. "Now if I was to make breakfast, son, I would be depriving you of a learning opportunity. I can't have that on my conscience.

"Maybe I can give you a few pointers, though. First, your fire is too hot." Red Dog knocked apart some of the glowing coals with a long stick. "Second, while we're giving that a minute to cool, you might want to thin that batter with a little water. Unless you want to mass produce hockey pucks."

Brad did as he was told. Red Dog's lazy drawl and easy nature took the sting out of his teasing. After thinning the batter, Brad poured half a ladleful on the griddle.

"Hear that?" Red Dog asked. He closed his eyes and nodded with a satisfied sigh. "A peaceful, gentle hiss, not an angry sizzle. No batter sputterin' and hoppin' and scorchin' over the place. Now you got 'er tamed."

Brad waited a few moments and then flipped over the pancake. Golden brown. "How about that, huh?" he said proudly. "Look at this one, guys. Am I a cook or am I a cook?"

"That's a tough one. Could you repeat the question?" said Brad's friend Lance, as he staggered out of their teepee, buttoning his shirt. Darin followed close behind Lance, rubbing his eyes sleepily.

"Your turn to cook tomorrow, Lance," Brad said. "Watch the master and learn."

"Tomorrow we have eggs," Red Dog said.

"I'm pretty good at eggs," Darin piped up.

"Music to my ears," grinned Red Dog. "You're on for breakfast tomorrow, Darin."

"First pancake coming up!" called Brad. "Bring the plate."

So far, Brad thought, Camp Grubstake had been just as advertised. He loved the adventure of the pioneer setting: no cabins, no motorized vehicles—everything hauled by horse-drawn wagon. Last night's campfire was fun. Sleeping out in a teepee was fun. Cooking pancakes was fun. Scaring those girls was fun. The daily Bible study would be a small price to pay for such a good time. He chuckled to himself when he remembered Tanya Archer's reaction. Man, she jumped two feet off the ground!

Brad got so carried away with his success that he flipped the pancake up in the air. But it missed the griddle on the way down. It fell into the ashes next to the fire. Everyone laughed but Red Dog. Still holding the charred first pancake, Red Dog put his arm around Brad. "Son, I don't think you quite grasp what we're trying to accomplish here," he said in his calm, gravelly voice. "The object is to make that batter into something we wouldn't be altogether fearful to put into our mouths."

"Oh, I get it," Brad exclaimed, as if he had only just understood. "This is breakfast. We want to *eat* this stuff."

"Now you're with me," Red Dog said with a wink. With that he took an enormous chomp out of the charred pancake.

"Ughh! You are sick!" groaned Darin.

"I appreciate that, my boy."

"How can you eat that stuff?" asked Lance.

"I'm a counselor," Red Dog said, munching away. "I'm here all summer. When you're here all summer eating campers' cooking, you learn to eat such as this or you go hungry. As you can see," he said, patting his large stomach, "I don't like to go hungry. Now Bradley, how about filling the griddle up instead of one pancake at a time? We got a busy morning ahead of us."

"What are we doing?" Lance asked with a yawn.

"Riding horses for starters," Red Dog said.

"Alright!" exclaimed all eight boys of the Meadow Village.

Breakfast and cleanup took longer than Brad expected. They had to rub liquid soap on the outside of a pot so that the soot from the fire would scrub up quickly. Then they had to wait for the fire to heat the water hot enough for washing dishes. "Where is a microwave when you need one?" Brad groused.

But when at last they were ready to go, Red Dog called, "Fall in line, boys. We're off to the horse barn. Whoa, there!" He stopped and pointed to Darin's legs. With a cool wind blowing and the sun still hidden behind the ridge, none of the campers were wearing shorts except Darin. "Son, you might want to do your legs a favor and put on some pants. A saddle can rub bare legs pretty raw."

Darin licked his lips and stared at Red Dog. Brad wondered why the suggestion made Darin uncomfortable. "Nah," Darin said at last with a shrug. "I'll be all right."

"Suit yourself. It's your hide," Red Dog said. "Let's go."

"You sure it's okay to just leave everything here?" Darin asked. His eyes were normally deepset and narrow; now they looked like slits.

"No problem," said Red Dog. "Bears only come at night." Brad chuckled to himself, knowing Red Dog was kidding. There were no bears at Camp Grubstake.

"No, I mean, what about the kids from the other villages?" Darin asked.

"I don't expect any problem," Red Dog said. "But if you got valuables or a fat wallet, you probably want to take that with you. Or I'll be happy to keep them for you." No one accepted his offer.

A short time later they plodded down the trail on horseback in a single file behind Wrangler Rick. Brad rode a nervous, little brown pony called Skeeter. He had wanted a bigger horse. But when he saw the troubles Lance was having just ahead of him, Brad was grateful for his mount. Lance was stuck with a big red horse named Lord Godiva that kept stopping to eat grass. A wide gap opened up between Lance and the horse ahead of him.

"Pull harder on the reins," Brad said.

"I don't want to hurt him or get him mad," Lance said.

"He knows that," Brad laughed. "A horse can tell when he's got a wimp riding him. That's why he's being such a stinker."

The comment goaded Lance into being more forceful. When Lance finally urged Lord Godiva into a trot, Skeeter followed closely. Trotting was no fun. Lance was jangling like loose change in a pocket. Brad felt like his teeth were being shaken loose.

"Don't just sit in the saddle," called Wrangler Rick from the front. "Use your stirrups. Stand up in them and get the weight off your seat."

After some awkward efforts, Brad figured out what the wrangler was talking about. If he put his weight on the stirrups, his legs could cushion the shock.

Once he stopped jarring so much he could begin to look around and enjoy the ride. Wrangler Rick led them up a steep trail to the top of a ridge. When they reached an open meadow, the horses took off in an easy canter.

"Yee haw!" Brad shouted as Skeeter loped along close behind Lord Godiva's tail. From his perch atop the saddle, Brad could see rolling farmland and occasional barns stretching for miles off to the north. The woods to the south branched off into endless coulees and finger ridges.

While Brad was admiring the view, Lord Godiva discovered another tempting stand of grass. He stopped suddenly. Skeeter nearly ran right up his back. The horse stumbled and Brad had to grab the saddle horn to keep from pitching forward over his neck.

"Get that old junker off the road!" Brad scolded. "You're liable to get somebody killed."

"I want my money back on this ride," Lance said sadly, yanking on the reins.

They wound their way back down the ridge, following a wide trail lined with log steps to keep the soil from eroding. As they broke out of the woods at the foot of the valley, the land looked familiar. They were near their own Meadow Village camp. Brad looked back over his shoulder to see if he could spot their teepee further up the valley. Behind him, Darin did the same.

When they cleared a stand of shagbark hickories that clung to the ridge, Brad caught a glimpse of their gray teepee. As he was about to turn away, he detected some movement.

Darin saw it, too. "Hey, there's someone in our village!" he shouted furiously.

Two of the horses snorted and stamped nervously. "Don't holler like that," Wrangler Rick said, sternly. "You're scaring the horses."

Whoever was trespassing in their village must have heard the shout. A speck of red flashed behind the teepee and into the woods. Brad thought he saw another shape, maybe two, scurry into the brush.

"I wonder what that was all about," Red Dog said, scratching his beard. "Somebody got valuables they ain't told me about? Darin?" Darin did not admit to anything and neither did anyone else.

"When we get done riding, you fellas head back to camp and check your stuff over," Red Dog said. "You find something missing, let me know. If something's gone, I'll talk to Pat, the camp director, and we'll get this stopped quick."

Before he turned around in his saddle, Brad shot a last look at Darin. Brad never cared much for him. He knew from back home that Darin had a mean streak. Most of the time Darin was kind of quiet. But you never knew about him. Darin was a bit strange, and Brad never felt at ease with him. The nervous way Darin was biting on his lip and staring back at the camp made Brad even more uncomfortable.

Brad had only his clothes, sleeping bag, and his Bible in that teepee. Nothing anyone would be interested in stealing. Obviously, though, Darin had something else back at the teepee. Brad wondered what it was. What did he have that was so important? Did someone else know about it and want it badly enough to break into their teepee to get it?

That must be *some* secret he is keeping, he thought.

THREE

A New Flag

The trail along the flats back to the barn followed a winding, trickling creek. Twice the horses had to cross the creek. Brad was fascinated by the way Skeeter tested the water and then lurched across. That was the first time he realized how powerful these docile animals were.

But his enjoyment was squelched by an uncomfortable feeling. The one thing he had worried about when he had signed up for camp was getting stuck with some snotty kids who would ruin the whole week. After the calm first night he thought maybe he had lucked out. But now he was no longer sure. He wished he could figure out what was going on with Darin.

While Red Dog stopped to help Miller, the maintenence man, load the horse-drawn wagon with lunch for the villages, the rest of the boys rushed back to Meadow Village. On their way, Brad saw the girls from Forest Village sitting in a circle on the hillside. Probably a Bible study. Aha, one mystery solved! Brad nudged Lance. "Look what Tanya Archer's wearing."

Lance inspected her from a distance. "So? I see an ordinary shirt and blue jeans. What's the deal?"

"She's wearing a red shirt," Brad said. "One of those sneaks I saw at our village had a red shirt."

Lance nodded and smiled. "Mmmmm. You don't suppose someone was trying to get even for last night, do you?"

"That's just what I think," said Brad. He shot a glance at Darin. The kid was eyeing the girls with one of his sullen looks.

When the boys reached their village, they saw few signs that anyone had been there. The cooking and camp equipment appeared to be untouched. All the boys carefully shook out their sleeping bags just in case the girls had planted something like a frog in them. Nothing. Lance thought that maybe his duffel bag had been messed with—his clothes were not folded as neatly as he remembered. Brad thought his backpack might have been moved. Or maybe it was just where he left it—he couldn't remember.

But no one reported anything missing. Not even Darin. Brad watched him closely. Darin poked through his gear for a long time. But if something was missing he was not saying.

"I wonder what they were doing," said Lance. "Maybe Darin's yell scared them away just as they got here."

Brad dropped his duffel bag by the teepee wall next to his pillow. As he did, he saw a pair of pants crumpled next to his Bible. They seemed to be the faded purple jeans that Darin had worn the day before, although in the dark of the teepee it was hard to tell. He bent down to pick them up. "I think these are yours, Dar—ughhh! They're soaked!"

He dropped them on the grass inside the teepee and rubbed his hands on his shirts. The jeans were not dripping but every inch of them was wet and cold. And they were gritty with sand.

Darin stared at him in icy silence.

"Yep, those are Darin's all right!" Lance said with a laugh as he came over to Brad's side. He lifted up the pants. "Man, what did you do, Darin? Fall in the water?" Lance said, laughing. "Or did those girls do this?"

Darin stood silent for a few moments. "I went swimming," he finally mumbled.

"Go on!" Lance said. "When? We haven't had any free time yet."

"Last night," Darin said quietly. There was a challenge in his voice. He swaggered over and took the pants. "I felt like going for a swim."

"I thought I heard someone leave the teepee last night," said Matt, one of the three boys in the teepee whom Brad had never met before camp.

Brad stared at Darin, puzzled. "Why would you sneak out and do that at night? We'll get all kinds of chances to swim during the day." He shivered. "If it ever warms up, that is."

Darin shrugged. "I just felt like it."

"Come on," teased Lance. "What's the deal? You're hiding something aren't you? Come on, out with it."

Darin stood silently again. Anyone could see that he did not want to talk about it. Brad was ready to forget the whole subject. Just as Brad was leaving the teepee, though, Darin said, "Maybe I wasn't alone."

"Ooooh," said Lance. "This is interesting. It wouldn't have been anyone from, say, this teepee, would it?" Darin said nothing.

"Were you with a girl?" asked one of the boys.

"Maybe," Darin said.

"All right, who was it? Who was it?" said Lance, grinning. Brad glanced at Lance warily. Lance did not have enough sense to know when to back off.

While they waited for Red Dog to return, Lance kept pestering Darin. For a long time Darin just shook his head. Finally he sighed and said, "Okay, if I tell you, will you leave me alone?"

"Who was it?" gushed Lance, leaning closer.

"Tanya Archer," he said, slyly.

Brad gaped at him in disbelief. Tanya? He had known her since first grade. She was a nice girl. Smart, too—especially in math! Hardly the wild type. She was not all that popular and mostly hung around with a couple of girlfriends. Brad could not remember ever seeing her with a boy. He could not imagine her sneaking out to go swimming, unless it was with those goofy friends of hers. Now if Darin had said it was Courtney Blake, *that* wouldn't have surprised him.

On the other hand, Brad had just seen Tanya sneaking around their camp. That was not exactly tame stuff. This is weird, he thought.

By evening, though, a new event pushed any thoughts of Darin's midnight swim completely out of Brad's mind. The boys from Meadow Village had done their Bible study late that afternoon. They were the last to arrive at the old plastic-roofed outdoor shelter where campers from all the villages joined to eat their evening meal.

Hardly anyone was sitting down at the picnic tables, though. Most of them were gathered around the flagpole, clucking and laughing.

"Hey, look! They strung someone's grundies up there on the flag pole!" howled Lance. A white pair of boy's underpants was flapping in the breeze underneath the flag.

Brad laughed out loud. "Whose are they? I hope they're Red Dog's."

As Brad and Lance walked over to get a closer look, the crowd parted in front of them. People were pointing and whispering and laughing and giving them plenty of room. Brad had the uncomfortable feeling that, for some reason, he was the center of attention.

"Hey, nice undies, Brad!" called Ben, a younger boy from another village, whom Brad knew.

"Woooo! Woooo!" giggled the girls from Forest Village, staring right at Brad.

Brad stared at the makeshift new flag, his mouth hanging open. He flushed a pale shade of red. "Those are mine?"

"That's the rumor," sang Courtney.

"Rumor nothing! You were going through my stuff," accused Brad.

"In your dreams," sniffed Allison.

Brad felt his ears burning. So that's what they had been up to, he thought. They'd gone and embarrassed him right in front of everyone in the whole camp.

Clang! Clang! rang the dinner bell. The crowd broke up and dashed to their assigned tables. Brad walked slowly over to his table and plunked himself down next to Red Dog. The counselor was studying the flagpole.

"I don't know what the world is coming to when a man's shorts aren't safe from vandals," Red Dog said sadly. "Is nothing sacred anymore?" But Brad caught a twinkle in his eye.

"Now I know what they were doing in our village," Brad said. Part of him was angry, itching for revenge. This was going too far. This went beyond an innocent little jumping out of the bushes.

Or maybe it was all the same thing. Maybe they had a right to get back at him for that scare. Maybe he should just call it even. As he watched the camp director retrieve his belongings from the flagpole, he could not help but think that what they had done was funny, even if he had been the butt of the joke.

Why do I have to be so easy? he thought. How come I can't stay mad at people? Maybe that's why people like me. 'Cause I'm such a sap. But even that thought could not rekindle his anger.

"Look on the bright side," said Lance as he passed a plate of barbecued chicken. "At least they were clean."

Brad had to smile. "I'm just glad we saw them from the horse trail," he whispered to Lance. "It would kill me not to know who did it."

"So what are you going to do now?" Matt asked. He looked like a vulture eager for some more spoils of war.

Brad smiled dangerously. "Who knows? This could be a very interesting week." Privately, he had decided that he would not go looking for revenge. But if some opportunity just happened to come along, well, who could blame him for taking it?

FOUR

Rumors

The last guitar chord of "Kum Ba Ya, My Lord" faded into the night, leaving only the gentle rustling of the leaves and the crackling of the fire. Poke, the girls' counselor, let the quiet linger for a few moments. Then she blew on her fingertips like a gunfighter blowing smoke away from the gun barrel after a crack shot.

"Th-th-th-th- uh, that's all, folks!" she smiled. "These magic fingers have to get through the rest of the week. If I play any more tonight, they will be too sore to play tomorrow."

It was cold—unusually cold for a late June night. Tanya felt glued to the warmth of the campfire. She stayed seated even as others started heading for the teepee.

She was squirming, for a reason that had nothing to do with the knobby log on which she was sitting. The beauty of Allison's plan was supposed to be that they could get the underwear on the flagpole without anyone knowing who did it. Sure, the boys could have been suspicious. But there would be no proof. Allison, Courtney, and she could just deny it.

But Brad Walker *knew* they had done it. And she knew how he knew. She had heard the Meadow Village boys on horseback yelling just as she got to the teepee. Wrangler Rick *would* have to choose that trail today and come at just that time! The terrible luck shook her almost as much as the fright of the previous night. How could those boys possibly have recognized them from that distance for just that split instant they were in the open?

Great, Tanya thought. Now I won't be able to relax the rest of the week.

And if he doesn't turn the flagpole trick on us, he'll probably think of something worse. She had seen Brad scheming in hushed whispers with Lance Porter. Something was going to happen. She hated not knowing what or when. She would rather be scared without warning than go around in dread, not knowing when Brad would strike. Her peaceful week at camp was ruined. She would have to be on her guard all the time. Why did I let Allison talk me into that? We should have just let it go.

Snooping through someone's backpack had seemed exciting at the time. But now Tanya felt a little guilty over what she had done. She did not even know Brad well enough to even say "hi" at school. How would she like it if someone raided her stuff just like they had raided Brad's? What if someone put *her* underwear on the flagpole? In fact, they might.

As she thought about sneaking into the Meadow Village teepee, she wondered about that wet pair of jeans. They had not known which duffel bag was Brad's and so they had snooped for clues. Tanya had found those wet pants tucked in the edge of the teepee, behind a pillow. The cold wetness had surprised her so much she had thought it was a snake and had jumped back with a yelp. Those pants were not just a little wet; they were totally soaked and sandy, as if someone had fallen in the water. What was the story behind that?

"Coming in for devotions?" Poke asked quietly, gently jabbing Tanya with her trademark poke in the shoulder.

"Do I have to?" Tanya groaned. "It's so cozy out here." Devotions were awkward. They were not like Bible study—that was okay. In fact, even though she might not admit it, Tanya kind of enjoyed that. Poke was good at leading it. She talked about interesting stuff and they had gotten into a good talk about sin and temptation. But devotions were so personal the way Poke did them. That was the big problem with Poke—she was too serious, too open. Tanya was not ready for that.

Poke looked at her with those intense brown eyes. "Tanya, if you were a counselor, would you trust you to stay out here alone?"

"Sure," Tanya said with a shrug. "I'm not going anywhere. It's just so peaceful and warm here, I want to stay for a few minutes." Poke gave her a funny look, like she was trying to read something written deep in her soul. "What's there to do in the woods when it's dark, anyway?" Tanya finished.

Poke's thick eyebrows arched near her bushy bangs. "You wouldn't be tempted to, say, visit another village?"

After the flag-raising, their raid on Meadow Village had been no secret. "I guess we messed that up," she admitted. "We got carried away. It was just supposed to be a fun little secret. But I'm done with that stuff. Besides," she said, glancing anxiously into the darkness beyond the reach of the fire, "I sure wouldn't go anywhere at night. In fact, if you did leave me out here by myself, I'd probably get spooked and follow you right into the teepee."

Poke still had that funny look. "You wouldn't, say, take off and go swimming?"

Tanya laughed out loud. "Right! Look at me," she said, tucking her chin inside her jacket. "I'm next to a hot fire with a shirt, sweatshirt, and a jacket on, and I'm still cold. You couldn't *pay* me to go swimming."

Those brown eyes stayed serious. "Trust is important, Tanya. I want you to trust me, and I want to trust you."

"Sure," Tanya said. Now Poke really had her on edge. Tanya wished Allison and Courtney were there.

Poke stood up and backed away from the campfire smoke that had wafted over to her. "So there's nothing you want to tell me about last night?"

That was all Tanya could take. "What is it with you?" she said. "I don't have any secrets or terrible plans. Look, Brad Walker scared us half to death last night. We just wanted to get even. We did. That's done with. In fact, if I had it to do over again, I wouldn't even do it. I mean it—it's over." But she had a sinking suspicion it was not really over.

Poke scratched her head. "Tanya, I need you to come in for devotions now. It's important to me. Please?"

Tanya was baffled by her urgency. But she helped Poke douse the fire and followed her into the teepee.

In the pale glow of flashlights, Poke's serious face looked almost spooky. "I'm going to do something different tonight," she said. "Instead of a Bible verse, I want to talk about something. Do you know what the Eighth Commandment is?"

Tanya racked her brain, but one of the other girls beat her to it. "You shall not bear false witness?"

"Yeah," Poke said. "Do you know what false witness is?"

"Telling lies about someone," Courtney said, casually. She had been brushing her hair ever since Tanya had come into the teepee and showed no signs of stopping.

Poke nodded. "I think there's been some of that going on in this camp and it really bothers me. I've been hearing rumors that some girl or girls went out last night and went swimming with the boys."

Courtney gasped and giggled. Tanya went numb. Were people saying that about her? Was that what Poke had been getting at?

"I've heard that rumor from both boys and girls, and I've heard it from some in this teepee," continued Poke. "How many of you have heard it?" Tanya stared in horror as a half dozen hands went up.

"Wait a minute," said Tanya. "Is this about me? What did they say?"

"It isn't important who—" Poke started.

"If it's about me, it is *too* important!" Tanya insisted. "What were they saying?"

"That you went out swimming after midnight with Darin Chatfield," piped one of the girls.

"What?!" exclaimed Tanya, her voice cracking.

"That is *so* stupid!" said Allison in disgust. "Tanya was sleeping right between Courtney and me all night. Besides, she's so scared of the woods she wouldn't leave the teepee at night. Even if she knew where she was going."

"I know," sighed Poke. "We have to trust each other or we're not going to have a good week." She looked over at Tanya and broke into her first hint of a smile since their talk at the campfire. "I trust Tanya. And I think it's really uncool that people spread rumors like that. Those things can really hurt. So I just hope you don't do stuff like that, and *please* don't go around repeating rumors. Can we all promise that?"

There were mostly half-hearted nods. No one wanted to admit to being involved with spreading that rumor. "Good," said Poke. "All in all today was a good day. Let's just forget about that stuff now and finish the day up right with a prayer."

Tanya did not hear any of Poke's prayer. Her heart was racing. No way could she just "forget about that stuff." Brad Walker must have been behind all this. Boy, he worked fast! Of all the childish stuff!

Me out swimming at night with that dopey Darin Chatfield? she thought. This was really stooping low. This was down there with the worms and maggots.

Her hatred for Brad kept her awake for hours. She burned off so much anger that her sleeping bag felt hot even on one of the coldest nights of the summer. Why was Brad picking on her? The underwear trick was Allison's idea; how did *she* get off scot-free?

To think that she had been feeling almost sorry for what they'd done to him! The creep! What was the matter with people like that? So he was cute. So he was outgoing. So he was popular. Did that give him the right to spread lies about a person—disgusting lies? If God was on the ball he would strike people like Brad Walker dead with a lightning bolt! She wished she had never come to this stupid Camp Grubstake.

The next morning, the Forest Village girls stopped in at the arts-and-crafts shed. Tanya could outweave, outsew, outcrochet, outdraw, and outpaint anyone. Show her a craft and she could catch on to it faster than Santa's elves. She finished weaving a beautiful rainbow belt out of yarn while Courtney and Allison were still struggling with the technique. The fact that she was still smoldering from the night before pushed her even faster than usual.

Normally the campers would have been working outside. But the morning was cold, with the sun buried beneath blankets of thick clouds. Not bad weather for running around or hiking. But for sitting and working with their hands, everyone preferred to be indoors out of the breeze. The craft shop was so tiny that Amy, the crafts director, was tripping over legs trying to get around to those who needed help. Having finished her project, Tanya stepped outside to relieve some of the congestion.

That was a mistake. She almost ran straight into Brad Walker, who was jogging down the hillside. Clenching her teeth, she turned her back and started to walk the other way down the road.

"Hey, Tanya. A little chilly for swimming last night?" Brad called.

The nerve of some people! You couldn't just shut up! Tanya thought. As if you haven't already done enough damage. She clenched her fists and hoped that if she ignored him, he would go away.

He didn't. "What's the matter?" he said, coming closer. As if he didn't know. "Tanya, you don't have to sweat it," Brad said with a laugh. "I'm not going to do anything to you. I admit, you got me good. You got me back." He came around her right shoulder where he could finally see her face.

"You're not still mad are you?" Brad said. "Come on, *I'm* the one who should be ticked off. You had no right to snoop through my stuff. But I'm not making a big deal of it. Don't turn this into a big boy-girl feud. If we start that, there are some crazy guys in my tent who could really cause trouble. Let's just call it all even."

Tanya stopped and turned to him. Her voice quivered. As much as she tried to prevent it, tears spilled out of her eyes. "Oh sure!" she said, her voice full of venom. "You spread your filthy lies about me and then come here with your, 'Oh, Tanya, let's call it all even. Let's be friends,' " she said in a mocking voice. "You're nothing but scum, Brad Walker!"

"What are you talking about?!" said Brad, his mouth hanging open.

Boy, what an actor! thought Tanya. He looked so innocent, shrugging his shoulders with his arms outstretched.

"You know what I'm talking about!" Tanya snapped.

"Honest, I don't," Brad insisted.

"You and that scuzzball Darin."

"Darin? Wait a minute. You mean you didn't go swimming with him that night?" Brad asked.

"Of course I didn't go swimming with him and you know it!" said Tanya. "But you thought it was cute to spread that rumor about me, didn't you? And now we're supposed to be even!"

"Tanya!" said Brad. Either he looked concerned or ashamed, Tanya could not decide which. At least he was not acting like it was funny anymore. "I didn't spread any rumor. I never said a thing. Darin was the one who said it."

Darin! That made it worse. It was stupid and childish to make up rumors about someone else. But for that ugly creep Darin to go around saying that she had gone swimming with him all alone after midnight! He was sick. Her previous hatred of Brad had been a flickering match compared to a bonfire of hatred that burned for Darin Chatfield.

"Why did Darin say that?" she said, menacingly.

Brad gulped and shrugged. He seemed confused and uncomfortable with the way things were going. "I don't know. Yesterday morning we saw his jeans were soaked from swimming." Tanya's anger cooled for a second as she thought about the pants. Hmmm, so that's what the deal was.

"We asked him about it," continued Brad, "and he didn't say much at first. But he finally said he'd gone out swimming after midnight and that you had gone, too. I didn't know whether to believe him or not, but I don't know why he would say that. Does he like you or something?"

"I don't even know the creep," Tanya snapped.

"Anyway," said Brad. "I'm glad we got that cleared up. Now maybe things will settle down."

"Oh, it's cleared up, is it?" challenged Tanya. "I'm just supposed to let that dork get away with saying that about me? He had half the camp believing it."

Brad raised his hand to calm her. "Don't worry. I'll spread the word. No one will think you went swimming with Darin."

"And then we're even, huh?" scoffed Tanya. Underneath her anger, she was surprised at herself for talking this way to Brad. She did not normally say much to boys, especially not one as popular as Brad. As upset as she was, she could see that it really was not his fault. And he had been more than fair about the flagpole business. But she could not stop herself. "I don't call this even." She turned and stomped back to the arts and crafts building. Allison and Courtney were standing in the doorway, whispering and looking at her.

"Tanya, wait." He moved up close to her. "Don't start messing with Darin. He can be bad news. I don't think he's going to take things the way I did."

No, of course not, Brad, she thought. You're just so perfect. No one would ever take things as calmly as you. Would they, Mr. Perfect?

"Don't tell me what to do!" Tanya said, and rushed away to join her friends.

Pony Express

C an you find another gear there, Darin?" called Red Dog to the boy who trailed a good fifty feet behind the group.

Darin was really dogging it, Brad thought. The kid looked like he had spent two days in the desert without water. Even though it was late in the morning, Darin's normally slitty eyes were puffy and crusted over with sleep.

Darin made no effort to move faster until Red Dog said, "I see an earlier bedtime coming up for someone."

"Why do we have to go on this stupid hike?" Darin grumbled, forcing his legs to move up the hill a little faster.

"To help you appreciate the wonderful world God put you in," said Red Dog.

"I appreciate it," moaned Darin. "Can I go back now?"

"Son, how can you appreciate what you don't even know?" scolded Red Dog. "This hike will help you to know a little more about your neighborhood."

"Welcome to another episode of Mr. God's Neighborhood," Lance quipped. He was not fond of hiking either. Matt and some of the others loved it, though, and were crowding around Red Dog. They not only listened to all his comments but even asked questions. Brad could go either way. Normally he was not big on hiking unless it included rock-climbing and tree-climbing and gulley-exploring. This follow-the-counselor stuff was pretty tame. On the other hand, he liked being out out in nature. The open spaces and the quiet helped settle his mind. They were a nice break from all the goofy problems down in the camp villages. Standing on a sandy ledge halfway up the ridge, Brad felt far out of reach of Tanya and her friends and whatever plots they were hatching.

"Anyone know why the trees are so sparse and scrawny on this hill?"asked Red Dog.

"Because they're wimps?" said Lance.

Red Dog was unflappable. "Why are they wimps?"

Lance shrugged.

"Notice how this ridge is much warmer than the one we started off on by our village?" Red Dog asked. "Why is that?"

"That's simple. This side is in the sun and that side is in the shade," Brad said.

"Simple as that may sound, you're on to something there, son. This is a south-facing slope," explained Red Dog. "The sun scoots across the southern part of the sky. That means this slope stands directly in the hot sun almost all day. North-facing slopes slant away from the sun, so they are in the shade most of the day. Could that explain why the plants here are so different from those over there?" He pointed across the valley.

"Yeah," said Matt. "Too much heat, not enough moisture. It's more like a desert on this side."

Red Dog extended his hand for Matt to slap. "You nailed that one, son."

Hmmm, Brad thought to himself as he studied the two ridges. I never noticed that before. South-facing slopes and north-facing slopes—they really are different. How could a guy live for fourteen years and not notice that?

Darin was apparently going to live a lot longer without noticing. He had fallen behind again. There he was plodding along, head down, lost in his own thoughts. He probably didn't hear a word that Red Dog said.

"What's this plant?" Matt asked, pointing out a flat swirl of soft, almost fuzzy, light green leaves.

"That's mullen," Red Dog said. "In about six weeks it will shoot up a stalk about four feet high. The Indians used this plant for tobacco. What about that plant next to it? Anyone know that one?" It looked like an ordinary weed to Brad. "That's called chicory. It gets brown and dry in the late summer. The Indians used to make a kind of tea from that."

"Must be nice to know what all these things are," Brad marveled. He could tell a few trees by their leaves, and a few other things like cat tails and stinging nettles, but that was about it. Halfway through the hike he had added mayapples, columbine, liverwort, and Virginia creeper to his store of knowledge.

"Red Dog?" asked Matt, as they wound their way through a more heavily wooded section of the ridge. "Can we sleep out under the stars tonight?"

That sounded like fun to Brad. He was pleased to hear Red Dog say,"I like the way you think, son. Nothing like getting rid of a roof and walls at night to get you to feel for nature. Sure, I could see doing that."

Darin, who had not paid much attention to anything else Red Dog had said, heard this comment even though he was a good fifty yards back. "Isn't it kind of cold sleeping out?" he called.

"Last night would not have been a choice night," Red Dog agreed. "Would have had to pry your frozen carcasses out of your bags this morning. But if it keeps warming up the way it has this morning, we'll be okay." Darin scowled his usual scowl.

By the time they came down off the ridge, Brad's feet ached. He was tired of walking and tired of learning. The names and features all began to blur in his mind. Lance and he got in a silly mood as they trudged back toward their village for lunch.

"Anyone know what this unusual specimen is called?" Brad asked, bending over and poking at a piece of black string lying on the ground.

Lance pondered it a moment. "I believe the common name for it is 'black string.' The Indians used it to tie up their old newspapers. There is also a white variety that they used to clutter up their junk drawers."

When they reached the village, Lance began gathering kindling for the noon fire. "Where's Red Dog?" he said, as he arranged small twigs and splinters loosely over some discarded candy wrappers. "It's warming up so fast that I want to go swimming."

"He's back there walking with the human tortoise," Brad said. Red Dog and Darin had fallen so far behind that they were only just now turning into the valley that led to Meadow Village.

Brad sat at one of their two picnic benches, facing outward and enjoying the warm sun while Lance lit the fire. Lance was right. The weather had really changed. A swim would feel good. Anytime Brad thought of swimming, though, that whole mess with Darin and Tanya came to mind. Brad tried to shove it out of his thoughts. People want to get all hot and bothered over stuff, that's their business, he decided. I'm out of this one.

Red Dog and Darin had finally ambled to within fifty yards of camp when Brad heard the rapid drumming of horse hoofs. Wrangler Rick was galloping up the valley, one hand holding down his cowboy hat to keep it from flying off his head. "Pony Express!" called Rick. "Delivery for Meadow Village!"

He pulled up next to Red Dog and slung a small pouch to him. With a tip of his hat, he wheeled and galloped back down the valley. Red Dog thumbed through the pouch. He handed a letter to Darin and pulled out two for himself. Darin ripped open his letter and stuffed the envelope in his back pocket. As he read, he retained his usual scowl so it was hard to tell if it was good news or bad.

"Who's it from?" Brad asked.

"Home," Darin said, with a look that added, "none of your business."

"Mail call, boys," Red Dog announced for the benefit of those in the teepee. "Lots of letters today. Read 'em and weep," Red Dog said, handing the pouch to Brad.

Brad filed through the stack, not allowing his hopes to get too high. He was hoping his mom or dad or one of his sisters would write. But it was still early in the week. Oop, there was one addressed to him. The handwriting did not look familiar. Brad wondered why there was no return address. Come to think of it, there was not even a stamp on it. Puzzled, he tore it open and began to read.

> *Dear Brad,*
> *How are you doing, my dear little pea-brain? Boy, were we glad to dump you at camp and get you out of our house for awhile. You know we love you very much but you're such a complete moron that none of us can stand you. I know that doesn't sound good but you know what I always say: honesty is the best policy. Hope you're having fun at camp and aren't embarrassing us by making a fool of yourself. Think about changing your underwear at least once this week. And hey, your breath is so bad I can smell it from here. Didn't you pack your toothbrush?*
>
> *Love,*
> *Dad*

"What is this?" Brad yelped. He looked again at the envelope with no stamp and no return address.

Lance swore as he finished reading his letter.

"Clean it up, Lance," said Red Dog. "You're polluting this wonderful, pure camp air."

"But look at this!" Lance sputtered, showing the letter to the counselor. "My dad wouldn't write garbage like this!"

"You got one, too?" said Brad, crumpling his letter up in disgust. "No stamp on it, I suppose?"

"Gee, I didn't even look," Lance said. He flipped the envelope over and nodded. "No stamp. These didn't come through the mail." He exchanged a cold, knowing look with Brad. "Somebody in camp wrote these and dumped them in the mail pouch."

"Yeah, I wonder who," Brad said, sarcastically.

Red Dog gave the letter back to Lance and took the one offered by Brad. "You know what I think, boys? I could be wrong but it appears to me that someone in these parts hasn't quite caught the spirit of Camp Grubstake. Did all you gentlemen get a letter like this?"

All the others angrily displayed their letters, except for Darin.

"You didn't get anything like this, Darin?" Red Dog asked.

Darin looked at the note Matt showed him. For a second he looked bewildered. But then Darin spat and muttered, "Yeah. I threw it in the fire."

"I thought you said that letter was from home," Lance said.

"It was a stupid letter," said Darin. "I wasn't going to pay any attention to it."

"It's Forest Village," Lance said. "They've been soreheads ever since we scared a few of them the first night." Out of the corner of his eye, Brad saw Darin sneak a look at the envelope hanging out of his pocket.

What was it about Darin anyway? He kept reminding Brad of a "what's wrong with this picture" exercise. Brad had a gnawing feeling that Darin had a secret behind almost everything he did. But Brad could not put his finger on what. The mystery was driving him crazy. Brad found himself spending a lot of time studying Darin for clues.

Brad thought that Darin was a pretty good liar, mainly because Darin was so secretive. Had he been lying when he had said the letter was from his family? Why wouldn't he show his letter to the rest of them if he thought the girls had written it? Especially since he seemed to enjoy playing up the feud between the villages. Did Brad imagine that brief look of confusion on Darin's face when the others started talking about their letters? And he had seen Darin steal a look at the envelope. Why? To see if there was a stamp on it? If he had to do that, he must not have noticed before that there *wasn't* a stamp on it. Maybe he actually thought it had come through the mail.

He couldn't have thought that was a letter from his dad, Brad thought. I wasn't taken in for an instant. I mean, that's so unlike anything a dad would ever say. A horrid thought came over him. What if some dads really did talk like that to their sons? In that case the letter wouldn't have sounded so fake, would it? *Were* there really dads like that? Brad didn't want to think about it.

"Gather around here a moment, boys," Red Dog was saying, pocketing one of the letters. "I'll take care of this. I'm going to have a little discussion with the counselor over in Forest Village and put a stop to this foolishness. You guys leave it alone, okay? Practice a little Christian forgiveness. I'm going to ask them to knock it off and I want you to promise me you won't go pullin' anything. Are we clear on that?"

Brad nodded but he had mixed feelings about the whole episode. Forgiveness? No problem. He knew how upset Tanya was and why. He was not at all surprised that she had tried to get back at Darin. Why the rest of them got letters was beyond him. Unless the girls thought they were all great friends with Darin. If this was the worst they could do, no big deal. It was so dumb. Tanya must have been so mad that she was not thinking straight. Like a few phony insults were supposed to hurt!

He wasn't so sure about leaving it to Red Dog, though. Yeah, Red Dog would handle it and get all the nonsense stopped. But it almost felt like the boys were running to their moms to protect them. Like they couldn't handle their problems by themselves. With this and the flag-raising, Brad had taken a couple of shots now without defending himself. He did not want anyone thinking he was a wimp. Those girls had better not push their luck any further.

Truce

W hat crazy weather, thought Tanya. Early this morning she had been too cold to sit down and eat her breakfast. Even standing up she had been able to eat only a few bites of granola. The milk was too cold to drink, the spoon was too cold to pick up. But now she was lifting her long hair off her neck to help her cool down. They should have played volleyball first thing in the morning to warm up rather than waiting until the late afternoon heat.

"What's the score?" asked Courtney. She was standing behind the serving line on the far side of the net.

"We don't have to keep score," said Poke. "We can just have fun playing."

"Five to seven!" shouted Allison. "Come on, serve it!"

Tanya smiled to herself. She knew how Poke's noncompetitive ways grated on Allison. At Poke's insistence, they had played for a while under Poke's no-scoring rule. Allison had been so bored she had finally pleaded with Poke for just one real, competitive game. Whether it was volleyball or checkers or racing to the bus stop, Allison played to win. She was the best athlete of all the girls in their school so she did not lose often.

Courtney swung limply at the ball. Her serve did not even reach the net, much less clear it. Tanya was not surprised. Courtney cared too much about her clear-polished fingernails to risk breaking one on a hard serve.

Now Tanya moved over to serve. "Seven-five," she called and lofted a high serve over the net. She had meant to keep it away from Courtney so as not to embarrass her. But no matter how Tanya tried to aim the ball somewhere else, it seemed to wind up falling on Courtney. Courtney backed away from the ball and half-heartedly pushed at it with one hand. She missed.

While a few teammates glared at Courtney, Courtney glared at Tanya. Poke stepped in and scooped up the ball. "This is just a game. We're supposed to be having fun, remember?"

Tanya aimed her next serve so far away from Courtney that it sailed out of bounds.

"What's the score?" asked the next server on the opposing team.

"Five-eight," Allison called. Tanya heard her grumble under her breath, "Am I the only one who knows how to keep score?"

Several minutes later, Tanya chased after a ball hit far beyond the end line. As she finally stopped the rolling ball with her foot, she saw a group of boys walking from Meadow Village. They were wearing swimsuits and were flapping and snapping their beach towels at each other. The sight made her even more aware of the heat. A swim would sure feel good! Maybe they could go down to the swimming hole after their game.

No, that wasn't such a good idea, she realized as she jogged back to the courts carrying the ball. Not if the Meadow Village boys were going to be there. She hated Darin so much she couldn't stand to be in water contaminated by him. She wanted to avoid the other boys for a different reason. Those letters.

Tanya had happily written that poison-pen note to Darin. It had felt good. Her only regret was that she hadn't said even worse things to the creep. The other letters had been Allison's idea, naturally. According to her, all of the boys from Meadow Village had been involved in spreading that rotten rumor, so they all deserved a little something. Most of the girls had gotten into the act, writing nasty letters to each of the boys, supposedly from their parents. They had all thought it was a big joke. Most of them laughed hysterically as they came up with insulting things to say.

Tanya had been too concerned with her own letter to Darin to say so, but she thought it was kind of dumb to write to *all* the boys. Darin deserved it, the creep. (She could not even think his name any more without adding "the creep.") But why do it to anyone else? The girls had already gotten Brad Walker good, and he had been a sport about it. Tanya believed him when he said that he wasn't planning any revenge. The girls should have considered themselves lucky they had gotten away with it.

They should have just ignored Meadow Village. Except for Darin. The creep!

Tanya's team was two points away from an easy victory when Allison nodded her head to the right and rolled her eyes. Tanya immediately saw what she was signaling. The Meadow Village counselor was nearing the court. He was wearing moccasins and navy blue swim trunks, and he had a towel draped over the right side of his huge chest. They called him Red Dog, but he looked more like a grizzly bear to Tanya. He stood by the net, smiling, until Allison finished off the game with two overhand serves. Poke approached Red Dog and jabbed a playful finger in his shoulder.

"What's up, mystical red one?" Poke asked. "Want to join us?"

"Maybe my boys can join you for a friendly game later this week," Red Dog said, cheerfully. "Then again, it might not be a friendly game." He pulled an envelope out of his back pocket. "Junk mail has struck Camp Grubstake."

Poke took the envelope and glanced quizzically at Red Dog. The Forest Village girls were suddenly very quiet as Poke read. Tanya retreated behind Allison who was calmly dribbling the volleyball.

Poke screwed up her face in disgust. "Oh. No. No," she commented as she read. "What is this?" she asked when she finished. "You don't really think a parent would write garbage like this?"

Red Dog shrugged, "There's strange people out there. Fact is, though, a parent *didn't* write this. Look here, no stamp. This letter didn't come from outside this camp."

"Well, this stinks," said Poke. "But what—"

"This wasn't the only one," Red Dog interrupted, sizing up the girls who were milling around on the court. "All my boys got mail today. They don't have much doubt about where it came from. I thought you might be interested, seeing how it's not the kind of class assignment you normally give."

"Can we go back to the village?" asked Allison casually. "We're done playing. It's hot standing around in the sun."

Boy, she knows how to play it cool, Tanya thought. This whole thing is her fault and she is the only one who doesn't look guilty. If she just would have let Tanya write that one letter and left it at that, nothing would have happened. Darin probably wouldn't have shown the letter to anyone. He just would have read it and gotten what he deserved. That would have been the end of it. And even if he did show it around, what's one letter?

No big deal, right? But a whole village gets bogus hate mail and you think no one's going to notice? Bright move, Allison, Tanya thought.

"Hold on," said Poke, deep in thought. "What makes you so sure my girls did it?"

"Me, I had no idea," said Red Dog. "My boys had a good hunch. Right now, though," he continued, surveying the group, "I'd say the air is so thick with guilt it's a wonder we can breathe. Don't take my word for it, though. Ask your girls."

Poke sighed. Everytime she looked at the letter, a fresh jab of pain shot through her. "You don't suppose your guys did anything to, I don't know, provoke this?"

Red Dog smiled. "Wouldn't surprise me. We aren't all angels up there at Meadow Village—none of us. Look, I'm not making a federal case out of this. In fact, you can burn the letter. All I'm sayin' is that whatever's been goin' on between these two villages better stop before this gets uglier than it already is. My boys have promised to leave your girls alone. If your girls promise to leave us alone, hey, I'm a happy camper."

"Sure. Well, thanks for showing me this, Richie," Poke said. "If my girls did it, I apologize. I guess maybe I need to talk with them a bit, first."

"Sure. Good afternoon, ladies," Red Dog said. He slowly walked off to join his campers at the swimming hole.

"Okay, time out," Poke said, putting one hand perpendicular over the other. "What about these letters, gang?"

Tanya glanced around and saw that everyone else had suddenly become very interested in the ground, their shoes, their fingers—anything that gave them an excuse not to look Poke in the eye.

"I guess I'm not much of a counselor," Poke said, sadly. "If this is how much we trust each other."

All of a sudden Allison looked up defiantly. Tanya knew what she was going to say. Just as the words, "I don't know anything—" spilled out of Allison's mouth, Tanya jumped in with, "It was *my* fault. The whole thing was my idea." She was not sure why she was taking the rap for this whole business. All she knew was that Allison was liable to make it worse by denying everything.

Poke walked over to Tanya. "It's about that midnight swimming business, isn't it?" she said quietly. Tanya nodded, biting her lip. Smiling weakly, the counselor gave Tanya a poke in the shoulder. Then she put her arm around her and squeezed her. "Tanya, Tanya," she said. When she finished her hug, Tanya saw that Poke was misty-eyed. Tanya could not helped but get a little choked up, although she was not sure why. She had been expecting to get chewed out, and here she was getting a hug. "Tanya, I know it's tough when people do dirt to you for no reason," Poke said, looking her square in the eye. "But you don't really think this is the answer to it, do you?"

Tanya shook her head. No doubt about it. She had known from the start that the letters were a dumb idea—except for the one to Darin. Now she felt kind of low and dirty for stooping to even that. Although he deserved it. The creep!

"Enough of this garbage, already," said Poke, addressing the rest of them. "Meadow Village promised to stop. Same goes here, okay? Got it?" She stared one more time at the letter. Then she crumpled it up and tossed it in an open garbage can behind the volleyball court.

Tanya breathed a sigh of relief. A truce felt good. Maybe now they could just enjoy what was left of the week. No more fear and dread about what the boys were going to do. Some of Tanya's own anger had been blown away too. That also made her soul feel lighter, freer. Hating people was such heavy work, she decided. It just dragged you down and pinned you to the earth. She was determined not to even think about those boys anymore. Not even Darin Chatfield. The creep!

SEVEN

The Missing Sleeping Bag

Lance was the one who first noticed the missing item. He and Brad had stayed longer than the others at the swimming hole. The rest of their group had already changed their clothes and headed out to the "plastic kitchen" for supper. Except for Darin who was sunning himself on his blanket next to their teepee.

While Lance was zipping up his dry pair of shorts, Brad was still in his swimsuit, trying to shake water out of his left ear. Suddenly Lance turned to Brad with a puzzled look. "Where is Darin's sleeping bag?"

Brad looked at the bare, matted grass next to his own sleeping bag. He glanced behind Darin's duffle bag and pillow. Nothing there. He scanned the other side of the teepee.

"I already counted," Lance said. Brad's ear was still so plugged he could barely hear him. "Only eight sleeping bags in here, including Red Dog's. Where did he go with his?"

"Where did he what?" Brad asked.

"I said, where do you suppose Darin went with his sleeping bag?" Lance shouted loudly and slowly, the way Brad spoke to his nearly deaf great-grandmother.

With one last shake the ear popped clear. "Whew, that's better," Brad said. "Hey, I know," he said brightly. "We're sleeping out under the stars tonight, remember? Maybe Darin's getting a jump on us.

Probably put his bag out on the best hunk of ground before the rest of us could get there."

"But Darin said he wasn't going to sleep out tonight," said Lance.

Brad tried to remember the conversation. "You're right, he wasn't thrilled with the idea. But I don't remember if he said he absolutely wouldn't sleep outside with us."

"Let's ask him. He's right outside."

"What's your rush?" said Brad. "Let me get changed first."

They found Darin sound asleep on his beach blanket. Brad saw no sign of a sleeping bag anywhere. "Earth calling Darin. Earth calling Darin. Come in Darin," Lance called.

Darin woke with a start. "What's going on?" he asked, sleepily. "What time is it?"

Brad glanced at his watch. "About ten minutes until supper. Looks like you could have slept right through it." Darin yawned but did not respond.

"We were kind of curious. Any idea what happened to your sleeping bag?" Lance asked.

Darin picked himself up groggily. He brushed some grass and dirt off his towel. "What *about* my sleeping bag?" he asked, as if their question were just another in a weeklong series of nuisances he had put up with.

"Where is it, for starters?" Brad asked.

"What do you mean, 'where is it?' " Darin scoffed. "It's in the teepee. Where else would it be?"

"Guess again, pal," Lance said, cheerfully.

Darin's eyes narrowed to slits. "Oh, it's not there, huh? Like you didn't take it or anything," he said sarcastically.

"Hey, we just noticed that your bag wasn't in the teepee," said Brad. "We thought you might have already brought it out to get a good spot for sleeping under the stars."

"I ain't sleeping under the stars," Darin grumbled. He trudged off to the teepee, dragging his towel. After a brief search he turned to the others with a suspicious look. "All right. Where is it?"

"How many times do we have to tell you? We don't know anything," Lance said. "I just happened to notice the bag was gone."

More strange goings-on with Darin Chatfield, Brad thought. Everything that kid gets involved with turns out weird.

Darin tried to pat down a patch of hair that had dried funny during his nap. "So someone ripped off my sleeping bag, huh?" he said. "I wonder who!"

"Not Forest Village?" asked Lance.

"Oh no!" said Darin, his voice even thicker with sarcasm. "Those little angel dolls would never do nothing like that!"

"But Red Dog talked to them," Lance said. "He made them call a truce. They wouldn't dare."

"If they did take your bag—just supposing they did— then they must have done it before the truce," Brad said. He was hoping to avoid any more conflict.

Darin snorted and shook his head. "It was there when I put my swimsuit on. Besides, if they're going along with the truce, how come they haven't given me back my bag?"

Brad stared at him blankly. Darin had a point there. *If* the girls really took his bag. But Brad was not ready to buy that story yet. Who could believe Darin after that tale he made up about the midnight swim? At least Brad was pretty sure that one was a fib. "You didn't really go swimming with Tanya, did you?" he asked. "Tanya says it didn't happen, and I've never seen her so mad."

"So who can figure her out?" Darin said, wearily. "It was her idea to go swimming. I didn't even want to go. Now she pretends like it was just me. Just to get me in trouble."

That explanation really baffled Brad. Trying to figure out what was going on with Darin was like walking on ice. You couldn't take a step in any direction with confidence. Darin sounded like he was telling the truth. But then so had Tanya. Brad wondered if this was what it was like to be a parent settling little kids' fights. How do you know who to believe when two people swear to opposite stories?

"So what are you going to do?" Lance asked. "Tell Red Dog? I don't think he's going to be too happy about this."

"Nah, why get Red Dog all uptight?" Darin said. "He wants us to ignore those stupid girls anyway. So who cares about them? I'll act like nothing happened. They'll have to bring the bag back sooner or later. I'd love to catch them with the goods. If we keep our eyes open we can nail them red-handed."

"But until then what are you going to sleep in?" Brad asked. No way was he sharing his sleeping bag with Darin.

"No problem," Darin said. "It's warm tonight. Don't need a bag."

"You don't think Red Dog will notice you don't have a bag to sleep in?" Lance asked.

"Not if I stay in the tent while you guys are out there."

At that moment the sound of the dinner bell echoed through the valley. "Oh man," Lance said, "we better hurry! Those kids from Big Spring Village were late yesterday and they had to sing the table prayer all by themselves!" All three took off down the valley at a dead run.

As Meadow Village prepared for their campfire later that evening Red Dog announced a special treat. "You boys did a good job at Bible study today. I'm proud of you. In commemoration of the excellence shown I hereby declare this a s'more night."

"What's a s'more night?" Lance asked as he and Brad split some chunks of wood for the fire.

"It's a night when we eat s'mores," said Red Dog. "Hey, move your hand away when you bring that blade down, son. You might need those fingers some day."

Brad quickly pulled his hand off the wood.

"What's a s'more?" Lance asked.

"You serious?" Red Dog asked. "You've never had a s'more? It's a roasted marshmallow stuck between two graham crackers buttered with bear grease and onions. Great stuff."

"Yuk, it is not!" protested Matt. "You put the marshmallow in the cracker with some chocolate squares."

"Chocolate I can handle," said Lance. "Is this s'more business another one of those things the Indians used to do?"

Red Dog studied Lance with a deadpan look. Finally he said, talking to no one in particular, "I think the boy was actually serious. I can see we're going to have to spend a little more time on Indian lore around here. Now," he said, in a louder voice, "in order to roast marshmallows over a campfire, we'll need sticks. Long, green ones. You can each go out and find your own. The sun is starting to go down already so you best do it now while you can still see." As the boys began to scatter, he added, "And go off into the woods aways so you aren't stripping all the vegetation from around the village."

Brad sunk the hatchet blade as deep as he could into the chopping block and then grabbed his pocket knife. He enjoyed going off into the woods by himself. It made him feel like he was traveling back in time. With no other people around and no buildings or fences, he could imagine what it must have been like to have been the first person to explore the area.

He climbed up the hill behind the teepee. The trees there were mostly young and spindly. But they grew thick among the shrubs and bushes. Brad weaved his way up through the most-open sections.

"Watch out for poison ivy," Red Dog's voice sang through the trees.

Brad scouted around his feet for that familiar three-leafed plant. No poison ivy that he could see. As he studied the ground, though, he began to wonder if he were following a faint trail. Some of the ground plants and grasses were bent and crushed. A few thin branches were freshly broken. Maybe a deer went through here, he thought. Red Dog said there were deer in these woods, although they were more often seen in the spring and fall when noisy campers were not around.

The hill was so steep that Brad had to grab a small tree trunk to help him up. This ought to be far enough, he thought. Although he had probably climbed only fifty feet up the hill, he was puffing from the effort. He clipped off a tiny sapling at the base with his knife. He began whittling off the leaves.

To his right, the ground fell away into a narrow gulley. Brad saw that a large tree had fallen across the gulley. Many years ago judging by the thick blanket of moss that covered it. The deep shadows of dusk made it difficult to see, but Brad thought he saw a patch of red down there. Moving to a different angle he saw something even more peculiar. A black, charred mass seemed connected to the red patch.

Holding his marshmallow stick in one hand, Brad slid down the ravine on his seat. He stepped on the rotting tree trunk to get a better view. The odor of char and soot mixed with the heavy smell of fungus. What was this thing? It looked like it was made of some kind of fabric.

As soon as Brad picked up the red corner, he knew what he had found. The discovery stunned him. A sleeping bag! Darin's sleeping bag! Badly burned except for about an eight-inch square. The outer material had melted. The inner fabric was mostly gone. What was left was almost completely black and smelled so strong it made Brad cough. Only the zipper remained undamaged. Several thick charred sticks lay on the ground beside the bag.

Of all the strange things at camp involving Darin, this took the cake. Weirdness stuck to that kid like bugs on flypaper. Someone had not only taken Darin's sleeping bag but had burned it and then had hidden it in this remote ravine. What was going on?

Had Darin done this himself? Brad dismissed the notion as soon as he thought of it. Get real, he thought. What kid would torch their own sleeping bag? What would be the point? Darin was weird but he was not a maniac.

Brad thought about Tanya and how angry she had been that morning. She hated Darin, no doubt about that. He tried to picture Tanya stealing the sleeping bag and setting fire to it while the Meadow Village boys were on their hike. Tanya? He couldn't imagine her doing this no matter how bad she hated someone.

But then that's what all the neighbors say whenever someone goes crazy and starts shooting at people, Brad thought. "I don't understand it. He seemed like such a nice guy. No different from you or me." He had heard those comments on the news more than once.

By now the shadows of the wood had merged into dusk. Brad grabbed the unscathed corner of the bag and began hauling it up the ravine. One section broke off, but most of it came out intact. Brad dragged the bag down near the edge of the grass before he stopped.

He had intended to lug the stinking mess over to the campfire. Surely Red Dog had to be told. But then, this was *really* serious stuff—burning someone's sleeping bag. Someone could get in big time trouble for this. And with Darin, you were never quite sure what was going on.

Brad dropped the bag in the shrubs just at the edge of the clearing. This was Darin's sleeping bag. He should be the one to decide what to do about it.

EIGHT

War Council

Brad found Darin at the front of a line of boys waiting to impale marshmallows on their newly cut sticks. Brad waited. When his marshmallows were firmly in place, Darin moved toward the fire. Brad intercepted him.

"Darin," he whispered. "Come here."

"What for?" Darin said.

"I want to show you something," Brad muttered.

"I'm hungry. Wait till I'm done with this," Darin said grumpily as he bent down over the fire.

Brad could hardly stand to wait. He looked at the darkness sliding over the sky into the west. "I want to show you something. Quick, there isn't much daylight left."

Darin snorted. "So? Ever heard of a flashlight?"

"You ought to check," Brad snapped. "Maybe the girls took your flashlight, too!" Darin squinted at him suspiciously. Then without a word he stood up and set his stick on the picnic table. He followed Brad past the teepee.

Just before they reached the edge of the clearing, Lance came running up behind them. "What's going on? Don't you want to try those s'mores?"

At first Brad wanted to shoo Lance away. But then he decided he was glad to have Lance there. He needed another brain handy to help figure all this out.

"What's your big find, Walker?" Darin said.

"Nothing much," Brad said, reaching into the shadows. He lifted up the foul-smelling bag. "Recognize this?"

Just enough daylight lingered for the others to see what it was. "Oh, man!" gasped Lance. "Where did you find that?"

"Stuck back in the woods," said Brad.

Darin made no comment. Rather than stepping forward to examine the bag, he just glared at it.

Seeing the others' shock made Brad feel just a bit smug over his discovery. "Looks like someone mistook your sleeping bag for a marshmallow," he said. "Doesn't roast real well, does it?"

"Oh, man!" Lance said again. "Who did this? We have to show this to Red Dog."

"No!" said Darin, with sudden fierceness. For some reason Brad had expected Darin to say that. He was not sure why. Probably because the obvious thing to do was to tell Red Dog, and nothing with Darin ever went the way you would expect.

"What do you mean, 'no'?" said Lance. "Look at that thing. This is arson. It's destruction of property."

"Big deal. It's just a sleeping bag," said Darin.

"Are you nuts!?" Lance cried.

"Pipe down, would you?" Brad said, glancing back toward the campfire.

"This *is* a big deal," said Lance in a strangled whisper. "We're talking criminal charges here."

"It's just an old sleeping bag," Darin insisted. "It's full of holes. We were going to throw it away after camp anyway."

"Can you believe this guy?" Lance said. He was so amazed he was practically squeaking when he spoke. "You mean you're just going to act like nothing happened? Just let them get away with it?"

"Oh, no. I didn't say *that*," Darin said, in a dangerous voice.

Brad did not like the sound of that. People who go for revenge do something as bad or worse than what was done to them. Brad shuddered to think what Darin could do that was worse than burning a sleeping bag. This was no longer kid stuff anymore. The smart thing to do was let Red Dog take care of it. Now Brad was really glad Lance was with them. Maybe Lance could help him talk Darin into telling Red Dog.

"Let Red Dog handle it," Brad said calmly. "The counselors will find out who did it and make them pay."

Darin shook his head. "I don't care about the sleeping bag," he insisted angrily. "But nobody messes with me like this. Those girls have been messing with us ever since we got here, Walker. Hanging your underwear on the flagpole. Writing poison-pen letters. Now this. And we just let them do it! Like a bunch of sissies. We don't even fight back. What do we do? Tell Red Dog. Woo, aren't we tough! Come crying to Red Dog. And what does he do? Nothing. He asks them nicely not to do it again. They just laugh and think up something worse to do."

The last thing Brad expected was that Darin would be able to talk him into doing something. But that was just what was happening. Words like "sissies" and "babies" stung. Darin was right. The boys had turned the other cheek a couple of times and look where it had gotten them. The girls just kept getting more cocky. Maybe Brad should not have been such a good sport. Maybe if he had stood up for himself at the start and taught those girls a lesson they wouldn't have gone this far.

He struggled to resist Darin's tempting logic. "But what can we do?" he said. "I'm not going to burn anyone's stuff. And whatever we do, those girls will squeal and then we'll get be the ones in trouble."

"You can go cry to Red Dog when a bunch of girls pick on you, if that's the way you want it," sneered Darin. "But they mess with *my* property, they mess with me. I'm handling this myself. I'm not going to make a big stink. But I'm going to do something."

"But we promised Red Dog we wouldn't do anything," Lance said, doubtfully. He sounded like he was weakening, too.

"They're the ones who broke the truce," Darin said, pointing off in the direction of Forest Village. "The deal's off now."

Brad and Lance looked at each other silently, but it was too dark to see each other's eyes. Brad felt uncomfortable. Part of him was sure that they should leave the matter to Red Dog. But at the same time his pride was at stake. They had to do *something*. The whole village was being bullied by girls! If word got out, they would be the laughingstocks of the town when they got home.

"So what do you have in mind?" asked Lance, haltingly. "It better be good. I don't want to get caught and end up in major trouble."

Darin had no plan to offer. "I'll think of something," he muttered.

"Should we do it just by ourselves or as a whole village?" Brad asked with a heavy sigh.

"The more the merrier," said Darin with a humorless chuckle.

Brad thought for a moment. He was glad for the darkness now so the others could not see his hands shaking. He felt like they were walking on a tightrope. Oh, this was going to be tricky! They had to do something drastic enough to punish the girls. But man, they could get in serious trouble! He needed time to think this one through.

"Okay, let's meet back at the teepee during free time tomorrow afternoon," Brad said. "The whole village. Keep it quiet. Bring some ideas. We'll decide what to do then."

"Sort of like a war council, huh?" said Lance.

"I guess so," Brad said grimly.

The war council started out in chaos. Darin had just shown the rest of the boys the burned bag. Now everyone was so excited they were practically bouncing off the teepee walls. Most of their ideas were just as crazy as their actions.

"I know!" Matt shouted. "We catch a bunch of frogs and minnows and put them in their water jugs. They'll be so grossed out they'll be barfing all over the place."

Brad was trying hard to keep a level head. He had to think this thing through. "I don't think so," he said. "What if the fish die or have some disease or something? If the girls start getting really sick, we'd be dead meat."

"How about locking the girls in their bathroom," suggested Darin. "I know how to do it with pennies."

That's it? thought Brad. They'll scream and be rescued in a few minutes. Some punishment. They steal and burn a sleeping bag. We get even by locking a few of them in a comfortable bathroom for a few minutes? This guy never makes any sense.

That seemed to be the general opinion of the council. Darin's idea was hooted down without debate. "How about a raid?" said Max, one of the quieter boys in the village. "We could run in at midnight and knock over their teepee or throw water in their tent or something. We could be gone before they knew what hit them."

This was met with wild applause and war whoops. But Brad only groaned and said, "Look. If we do anything like that, they don't have to catch us to get us in trouble. Everyone will *know* we did it. Who else are they going to suspect? Then we're in trouble. Not only Red Dog but probably the camp director will get on our case."

His words sobered the group considerably. "But that's just the way it is, Walker," said Darin. "No matter what we do, they'll know it's us. We'll just have to pay the price. That's fine with me. It's worth it."

The furrowed brows around him told Brad that this was not so fine with everyone else. Nor was it fine with him.

"What's the point of doing something that will only get us in trouble?" said Lance. "They'll just be laughing at us all the more when we get punished."

"So are you guys wimping out?" Darin asked.

"Wait a minute!" Brad said. "I've got it!" A huge smile spread across his face. He rubbed his hands together and laughed. He jumped high in the air and slapped at the side of the teepee. "You won't believe this! It's absolutely perfect! I'm a genius! Those girls won't know what hit them! And no one will suspect us of a thing!"

Brad had to explain the plan several times before everyone understood what he had in mind. But by the time the war council broke up, all eight campers from Meadow Village were howling and laughing and high-fiving each other.

The plan was set to go off at midnight. It couldn't fail.

NINE

On Tanya's Shoulders

G et away, squirrels," said Poke. She stamped her foot at them. The furry gray raiders barely flinched. They kept munching and scattering the bird seed Poke had set out in her feeder. The ground below the feeder was a mess.

Standing with her hands on her hips in the morning light, Poke seemed smaller than usual to Tanya. Maybe it was because, for the first time this week, she was not wearing pants. Her blue gym shorts revealed how thin her legs were. The shorts were almost covered by an overlarge shirt that hung unbuttoned over her Camp Grubstake t-shirt.

Poke was too gentle with animals. The horses knew it, the squirrels knew it. None of them were afraid of her. "Here's how you get rid of squirrels," Tanya said. She found a couple of stones and fired them at the bird feeder. The squirrels dashed a few feet away and looked back.

"Hey, hey," said Poke. "Don't hurt them. They don't know they're not supposed to eat my seed." She studied the trees that bordered the village. "I've got a better idea. Let's hang the bird feeder on a line between two trees. That way the birds can get at it but the squirrels can't."

She found some thin rope and selected a couple of trees about twenty feet apart. "Squirrels can jump pretty high, can't they?" she said. "Tanya, are you a good tree climber?"

"No, I hate climbing trees," Tanya said. She did not really mind climbing but she hated heights.

"I like climbing trees," said Courtney. She had just emerged from the teepee, brushing her hair. She looked bleary-eyed, like she was having trouble waking up.

"You do?" Poke looked at her and then Tanya in surprise. Tanya smiled. Courtney had always been a climber. That always surprised people, especially those who knew how much she fussed over keeping neat and clean.

"What about your nails?" snickered one of the girls.

"Now that just goes to show you," Poke scolded the critic. "We shouldn't go around stereotyping people. Courtney, could you tie this end of the rope about ten or twelve feet up in that tree?"

"Sure." She swung into the tree like a little monkey.

While Courtney was fastening the rope, Allison announced, "Looks like we've got company."

Tanya turned toward the wagon trail. There was Red Dog surrounded by his campers. Someone else was with them, too. Someone with a familiar straw hat. Pat, the camp director. "Boy alert! Boy alert!" called one of the girls.

"Oh no!" gasped Courtney from her perch. "I look like a slob. I don't even have any make-up on!"

Tanya smiled. She may be a tree-climber but she's still the same old Courtney. "Too late now," Tanya told her.

"I'm not coming down," Courtney said. "I don't want anyone to see me like this." By "anyone" she obviously meant boys, and Tanya felt a little miffed at the slight. Courtney was being so ridiculous about this that she crawled higher into the heavier foliage of the tree.

Poke shuffled toward the visitors, her hands on her hips. "Good morning, gentlemen. And Madame Director," she called. "You guys are up early today. To what do we owe the pleasure?"

Red Dog scratched his beard. "I wish I could visit you under friendlier circumstances some time," he said.

Uh oh, thought Tanya. Now what? The usual twinkle in Red Dog's eyes had dried up. Pat was not smiling, either. But behind her several of the boys wore poorly disguised smirks.

Just then a branch cracked and Courtney screamed. "Ow! Ow!"

Courtney hung at an odd angle high above the ground. She was almost horizontal, with one arm clinging to a tree limb and her leg twisted. "Ow, my foot's stuck!" she whimpered. Poor Courtney, who had been so desperate to stay out of sight, suddenly had center stage. Two entire villages gawked at her from the ground.

"Now how did you do that?" Allison demanded, grinning broadly.

"The branch I was holding onto broke, and my foot's stuck," said

Courtney. Allison and Poke quickly climbed up after her. Allison tried to free Courtney's foot but it was wedged too tightly. Poke crawled out on a branch beneath Courtney. She tried to get close enough to Courtney to boost her back up to a vertical position. No luck.

"Let me try," said Brad. He climbed up past Poke. He tested the branch that Courtney was gripping. It was too weak to hold another person. Brad moved up to the branch above Courtney. He pulled himself along the limb and reached an arm down to Courtney.

"Don't look at me. I look terrible," Courtney whined, hiding her face.

Poke started shaking in silent laughter. Her branch started shaking and soon most of the tree was trembling. "Hey, cut it out!" yelped Brad, struggling to hold on to his perch.

"I can't help it!" Poke burst out. She laughed uncontrollably. "Courtney, you are too much!" she said. In an instant, the girls were laughing, the boys were laughing, even Tanya could not help it.

"Give me a break!" said Brad, desperately clinging to the branch. "You're going to make me fall!"

"I'm sorry," Poke gasped, trying to control herself. She climbed back down the tree and fell to ground, weak from laughter.

Brad finally coaxed Courtney to reach up with one arm. He caught her by the wrist. With Brad helping from above and Allison from below, Courtney managed to swing herself up to a vertical position. That took some of the pressure off her foot. Allison untied the stuck shoe. Courtney pulled hard and yanked her foot out of the shoe. She climbed back down the tree, looking like those crooks who shield their face from the television camera as they leave the court house. Allison wrenched Courtney's shoe loose and followed her down.

No sooner did Courtney hit the ground than she dashed for the teepee, hobbling on her twisted ankle. She was long gone by the time Brad reached the ground.

"I'm sure when Courtney recovers from the shock she will thank you," said Poke with a smile. "She wasn't prepared for gentlemen callers."

"Oh, was that Courtney?" joked Brad. "She told me not to look at her so I never saw who it was."

"Wouldn't it be nice if Meadow Village and Forest Village always showed that kind of cooperation," said Pat. The fiasco with Courtney had not softened the edge in the director's voice. Tension swept into the village like air rushing to fill a vaccuum. Pat meant business.

"Yeah, it would be nice," Poke said with a nervous smile. "I take it we have another problem."

"Last night someone raided Meadow Village," said Pat, severely. "They were quiet but they managed to do a lot of damage."

Tanya's eyes grew wide. It must have been pretty bad for the director to get involved. She looked at the boys standing behind Pat. Most of them had swallowed their smirks. They looked innocent or showed no expression at all. Lance Johnson's eye was swollen almost shut, and another kid had a large bruise on his forehead. She wondered what that was all about—whether it had anything to do with the raid. Darin was openly smirking. The creep! What was he up to now?

"The water jugs were all emptied," continued Pat. "Right on top of the firewood so the village could not get a fire going this morning. The clotheslines were cut. Swimsuits thrown into trees. A picnic table was dumped in the creek. Cooking pots were filled with mud. Garbage from one of the bins by the plastic kitchen was strewn all over Meadow Village. Would you or any of your girls happen to know anything about this?" Her tone of voice made clear who she suspected of carrying out the raid. Darin's smirk reappeared, wider than before.

Poke looked around at her girls. Tanya joined the others in shaking her head. "Pat, I'm quite positive that no one left our teepee last night," Poke said.

"You sure about that?"

"Look, I admit my girls did a couple of things earlier in the week that they shouldn't have," said Poke. "But we had a good talk about it and that's been cleared up. Every one of them promised they would leave Meadow Village alone, and I trust them."

Tanya was thankful they had Poke for a counselor. Given their track record this week, Poke could easily have wondered about them. Even though they had not done anything this time, they could be in big trouble if she were not sticking up for them. Tanya noticed Darin's smirk was fading.

Pat looked at Red Dog, who simply shrugged. After a long silence, Pat said, "I understand there's been a little battle of the sexes between these two camps. While I admit I haven't heard the girls' full side of the story yet, it seems obvious that Forest Village has been in on their share of the trouble.

"I'm not a detective," she went on. "I can't prove who did what around here. I do know that our campers have been given a great deal of freedom at this camp and that this freedom has been abused—more than once. Now since I can't prove who did what, all I can do at this point is make sure this kind of thing stops. So tonight, all campers will report to their villages directly after supper. They will stay there. All evening."

"But we have a trail ride scheduled for tonight," protested Allison.

"It's been canceled. At bedtime, each village will go to the bathroom in a group, accompanied by a counselor."

Tanya saw Darin's smirk give way to a scowl.

"One final thing," Pat said. "I'm sending an extra support staff person to sleep in each village tonight. Just as a precaution. This kind of behavior *will not go on*. Is that clear?" she asked, directing her gaze to both boys and girls.

"Yeah," said Poke, still bewildered. "Pat, I don't have a clue what went on at Meadow Village last night. But aren't you punishing the wrong people? I mean maybe you don't have much choice with the rest of us. But why punish Meadow Village if they were the ones who were raided? I don't like to see the victim punished."

"I guess you have a point," Pat said. "Okay, we'll make an exception for Meadow Village. Any other questions?"

There were none that anyone was willing to voice. Poke motioned to Red Dog, "Richie, can I talk you a minute?"

Pat started off alone down the wagon trail. The boys did not seem to know where to go. They just hung around waiting for Red Dog.

Tanya felt betrayed by the way Poke had stood up for Meadow Village. But she had to admit Poke had a point. She was about to head into the teepee to check on Courtney when Brad brushed past her.

"I hope you're satisfied," he said in a low voice and continued on a few steps past the cluster of girls.

Tanya followed him. "We didn't do it, Brad," she whispered. "Honest. It wasn't us."

"No kidding." Brad smiled a superior smile that told her he knew something she did not.

"What do you mean? Do you know who did?" Tanya asked.

"Maybe I do," Brad said with a chuckle.

Why do I ever bother trying to talk with these boys? Tanya thought, exasperated. They were all a bunch of twerps. "Then why are you just standing there letting us get punished for it?" she demanded.

"You're getting what you deserve," Brad said, coolly. "Maybe you're not getting nailed for the right thing. But it makes up for something else."

"You jerk!" Tanya was having trouble holding herself to a whisper. "Red Dog said you guys promised it was all over. You weren't going to do anything back. Truce, remember?"

"You broke the truce first. Admit it, you had this coming."

"We did not break the truce!" Tanya whispered angrily. "We haven't done anything to you."

Brad glanced around nervously. Obviously he didn't want anyone else hearing what he was saying. "Burning a sleeping bag is nothing, huh? Darin Chatfield isn't exactly a friend of mine, but he's part of our village. You mess with him, you mess with all of us."

"Come on, guys!" shouted Red Dog. He and Poke had finished their conference. "Back to the village. We have to plan our skit for tomorrow night's show."

Brad shot a smug smile at Tanya and jogged off to join his village. Tanya's mouth hung open. A burned sleeping bag! Darin's? Had everyone in Meadow Village totally lost their minds?! This was crazy!

She saw Darin approach Brad. That stupid smirk was back! All her previous hatred for Darin Chatfield poured back into her from wherever it had been bottled up, twice as strong as before. She clenched her teeth. She was so mad she could have bit through his spine if he was a little closer.

Allison called the girls together for a meeting during their afternoon canteen break. Tanya had already filled her in on her conversation with Brad. Allison related it to the others. "We're not 100 percent sure," she said. "But we think those guys trashed their own village just to get us in trouble."

"Why?" demanded one of the girls. "I thought we had a truce."

Allison's face wrinkled into a mask of pure hatred. She looked exactly like Tanya felt. "Darin Chatfield. He's been spreading more lies about the awful things we've done to him. Do you know what he said? He said we stole his sleeping bag and burned it!"

"You're kidding!" said another girl. "And they believed him?"

Allison nodded. "So we got stuck on probation for something they did. What are we going to do about it?"

The question made Tanya squirm. Always they had to "do something about it." Whatever they did always made it worse. And then the other guys would do something worse back to them. She thought of Poke and how disappointed she would be if they pulled something else after she had stood up for them. Tanya did not think she could stand letting Poke down.

But then she hated Darin so much. The creep! He really had it coming. If only they could think of a way to totally humiliate him without getting the rest of Meadow Village involved. And without being found out.

"I have a perfect plan," said Allison, rubbing an itch on her freckled nose. "We steal something out of the office. Something small but valuable. Then we plant it on Darin so he gets blamed for it. Hide it in his clothes or something."

Courtney laughed uproariously. Tanya felt sick. Stealing? This was really getting out of control. Sure she hated Darin but now they were talking crime. And what if they got caught in the act? No way could she go along with this.

"Too big a risk," she said. "They know we have it in for Darin and they'll probably figure out what happened."

"You've got a better idea?" Allison asked, miffed that her "perfect" plan was being rejected.

Tanya did not. But she felt she had to do something. "Look, Darin started this thing by picking on me so I've got more reason to get him than anyone. Let me handle it. I'll get Darin Chatfield, and I'll get him good. But let me do it my own way."

Allison didn't look convinced. "Are you sure you'll do anything? Or are you just going to back off?"

She knows me all right, Tanya thought. She *was* sort of hoping she might run out of time before her plan—whatever it might be—could be carried out. "Trust me," she said. "I hate that creep. I'll get him."

Allison and the rest finally agreed. Tanya felt as though she had avoided one deadly trap only to fall into another. Now it was all on her shoulders. What was she going to do about Darin?

TEN

Darin's Secret

Brad lay silent in his sleeping bag. He had woken up with a start, thinking that the teepee was about to collapse on him. But he had been only dreaming. The only sounds he heard were the heavy breathing of his fellow campers and an occasional snore from Red Dog. There seemed to be more light in the teepee than usual for the middle of the night. Brad wondered if the moon was out. Just to crush the last embers of doubt he had about the safety of the teepee, he reached out and touched the canvas. It was taut, firmly in place. Yep, only a dream.

Once awakened, Brad had trouble going back to sleep. The sneak attack on their own village had not gone as well as expected.

The plan had been for three of them to take part in the raid. Brad had figured that the odds of Red Dog hearing something and waking up would increase if more people were involved. Flashlights, of course, could not be used.

They had barely started their raid when disaster nearly ended it. Lance and Matt had run smack into each other in the darkness. They clunked so hard that Lance fell to the ground holding his eye. He was gasping and making strange little gurgling noises, trying desperately not to make a sound. Fortunately Lance and Matt recovered quickly. They had been able to finish the raid without being detected.

The next step had been to get Forest Village blamed. Red Dog had been easy to persuade. Brad thought they just about had the camp director convinced. But then Poke had thrown a wrench in the works. For some reason she had insisted her girls were not involved. That meant that everyone in camp ended up getting punished. Brad felt bad about that. He had not meant to ruin everyone's fun. Boy, if the word ever got out that Meadow Village had raided their own village, everyone in camp would be after their hides.

The plan seemed so perfect, Brad thought. It was supposed to solve the problem they had been having with the girls. But it had ended up causing twice the trouble.

Then Poke had to speak up in Meadow Village's defense and get that early curfew lifted for them. That *really* made Brad feel like a heel. It reminded Brad of a passage he'd heard in Bible study that morning. Something about being nice to your enemy because by doing so you would "heap burning coals upon his head." That was the phrase that stuck in Brad's mind. Man, burning coals on your head! He hurt just thinking about it.

It had seemed an awfully strange thing to say—one of those Bible verses that doesn't make any sense to kids. But now he had at least an idea of what it meant. Poke had done the nicest thing she could do for Meadow Village. And that was making him feel worse than any of the goofy little tricks the girls had played on him! Weird how that worked!

Then there had been that little chat with Courtney after supper. Courtney had insisted upon thanking him every chance she got and with far more praise than he deserved for helping her out of the tree. You would swear he had rescued her from the tower of the Dark Knight.

Brad generally tried to be pleasant to most people, boys or girls, unless he had a particular grudge. But you had to watch it with Courtney. If you so much as looked at her she took it as an invitation to go steady. Actually talking to her was asking for trouble. Rescuing her from a tree had put him in a real bind. Brad could see her lining him up in the crosshairs of her gunsights. Courtney could be kind of a fun person at times. She was not bad-looking, although it was hard to tell what was under all that makeup she wore most of the time. But Brad did not want to be anyone's boyfriend. Much less someone as boy-crazy as Courtney. I should have left her in the tree, he thought to himself.

He had gotten some useful bits of information from Courtney, though. She told him the girls knew what Meadow Village had done to their own village. Brad then asked her if the girls were planning any further revenge because of that early curfew. Courtney had cheerfully told him that it was not the boys they were mad at. It was that creepy Darin Chatfield. And oh, yes, Tanya was cooking up something for Darin. Tanya would not tell anyone just what she was up to. But Courtney assured Brad that it was a doozy. She seemed so eager to please that Brad did not doubt her for a second.

Brad was still mulling over how he was going to get away from Courtney now that he had let her too close when he heard a rustling next to him. He started to turn over in his bag and see who it was. But some instinct told him to stop. The noise was coming from Darin's area. He was still sleeping in his clothes, without a sleeping bag. The nights were pretty mild and he was able to get by with only a flannel shirt wrapped around him. So far Red Dog had not noticed the missing bag.

There was so much about Darin that Brad could not figure out. That business about the midnight swim on the first night. His strange reaction to the poison-pen letter. Brad was even beginning to wonder about the sleeping bag story. Maybe Tanya was a better actress than Brad gave her credit for, but she seemed totally bewildered when Brad had brought up the burned sleeping bag. Was that because she had not been expecting them to find it? Or did the girls really not know anything about that incident? And why did Darin insist that no one tell Red Dog about the sleeping bag?

No use asking Darin any questions. Darin always told as little as possible. If Brad was going to learn anything about his mysterious campmate, he would have to learn it by watching. If Darin was up to something right now, Brad's only hope of learning anything was to keep quiet.

Brad heard the muffled sound of someone working at untying the teepee entrance flap. Darin was going out! This was Brad's chance at last. Tonight he was going to follow Darin—spy on him.

He waited until Darin pushed through the opening before stirring. Quickly he jumped into his jeans and threw on a shirt. He thought about putting on shoes but decided there was no time. He peeked out of the opening. For a moment Brad thought he had lost his target. Thank goodness the moon was out! Brad caught a glimpse of Darin heading down toward the creek. He was carrying something in his hand; Brad could not tell what.

Red Dog snorted loudly. Brad's heart jumped. He shut the flap and ducked back into the darkness. But the counselor was still sleeping soundly. As silently as he could, Brad slithered out the opening and into the night.

Although the night air was mild, the heavy dew felt cold on Brad's feet. The moon shone directly on the front of the teepee. Brad dashed off to the shadows near the woods. From there he worked his way down to the creek, always staying hidden in the shadows. Once he snapped a twig and stopped dead, fearful of being discovered. He stepped on several sharp stones and branches. He even hit a thorn and hopped back, biting his tongue to keep from crying out.

Brad was afraid that Darin had gone somewhere else. But there was no way to move faster without being discovered. At last Brad drew near the creek. He heard quiet splashing amid the gurgle of stream water. There was Darin, standing half in the moonshadow of a willow only about thirty feet away. Brad watched him slip on a pair of jeans. He had the sinking feeling that Darin had already finished whatever he had planned to do. It looked like he really did go for midnight swims. Why?

But then Brad saw him pick up another pair of jeans. Darin bent over the edge of the creek and plunged the pants into the water. He swirled them around in the creek several times. Finally he pulled them back out and began wringing them out, starting with the legs. It was like watching a movie of some pioneer settlers washing their clothes in a river.

All at once it hit Brad what was going on. Could someone Darin's age be a bed wetter? Was that his secret?

There he was, washing out the clothes he had slept in. Brad *thought* he had smelled something as Darin was leaving the teepee. That was what he had been doing that first night, too. No wonder he was so secretive about everything. Brad could not blame him a bit. If it were Brad, he would die, actually die, of embarrassment if anyone knew.

As he took in the meaning of this new information, the strange things that had been happening in camp all week fell into place. The first night had been fairly warm so Darin probably had not slept in his sleeping bag. He must have been hoping the weather would stay warm all week so he would never have to risk using the bag. There had been an accident that first night. He had covered it up by doing exactly what he was doing tonight.

When his wet jeans were discovered, though, Darin had to make up a story to deflect suspicion away from him. The excuse: a midnight swim with Tanya.

Then the cold night. Darin had to risk using the bag just to stay warm. He lost the gamble. Suddenly he was stuck with embarrassing evidence that just would not wash away. What could he do but get rid of the evidence and hope no one noticed?

Lance had noticed that the bag was missing, though. Once again, Darin had to deflect attention away from himself. This time he took advantage of the war between the villages to cast suspicion on the girls. And I bought the whole story, Brad marveled.

What about the burning? Brad thought. He must have been desperate to keep that wet bag a secret. He could not take the chance of someone stumbling on it by accident. If anyone did they would immediately know what had happened. So he burned it. Of course that got blamed on the girls, too.

Boy, Darin was lucky that Poke had gotten the punishment lifted from Meadow Village. Pat had threatened to send another staff person to sleep with them that night. If that person was a lighter sleeper than Red Dog (and who wasn't?), Darin might not have been able to sneak out to do his wash. What would he have done then?

Brad came to two conclusions about Darin. First, he was one clever kid. Darin was making up most of this stuff off the top of his head. Yet it was good enough to fool the entire Meadow Village. More importantly, though, Brad realized what a terrible week Darin must have had. Imagine trying to get through a week covering up a secret like that. The guy always looked cool, but inside he must be a wreck. No wonder he seemed exhausted half the time. What's with this guy's parents? Brad wondered. How could they let him come to camp knowing the trouble he was going to have? Or maybe they made him come. That's even worse.

He thought he remembered hearing that bed-wetting was sometimes a sign of severe stress or emotional problems or something. He wondered if there was something going wrong in Darin's life. He could not help but feel that Darin must have had a tough life.

By the time Brad worked through all these thoughts, Darin was on his way back to the teepee. He passed fairly close to Brad, so close that Brad stopped breathing. At one point, Darin seemed to stop and listen. He kept peering around in the moonlit darkness.

Not until Darin reached the teepee did Brad relax. That relaxation lasted all of two seconds. Just long enough for Brad to realize that his odds of getting back to bed without Darin hearing or seeing him were poor. The moonlight was bright enough that Darin might see that empty sleeping bag next to him. What would Darin think if he suspected Brad had been spying on him and knew his secret? That was not a pleasant prospect.

Brad spent a few minutes trying to think of a way out of this problem. But his feet were cold and scratched and he could not stay out there all night. There was nothing to do but return to the teepee. As he sneaked back under the entrance flap, he could tell immediately that Darin was awake. Brad quickly found his sleeping bag. The downy softness felt soothing to his feet. That reminded Brad again that Darin was spending another night sleeping on matted ground with only a shirt wrapped around him.

Brad felt a hostile gaze. There was no sense in playing dumb, as though he did not know that Darin had left. Maybe he could bluff his way just as Darin had been doing. "Where did you go?" Brad whispered. "I couldn't sleep, so I got up to go for a walk. I saw you were gone."

"Went for another swim," Darin whispered back. "Where did you go?" Darin was an expert bluffer. Brad hoped he could match him this once.

"Just out," Brad said casually. "I didn't put my shoes on so I didn't go far. My feet hurt too bad. You shouldn't go swimming by yourself, you know. Especially at night."

Darin waited before answering. "How do you know I was by myself?" he asked with a hint of menace.

Brad felt his pulse quicken. "Who else could be out there?" he said. "All the other villages are wrapped up tighter than a prison tonight." Thank God he'd thought of that! Darin had almost trapped him. If this went on much longer he was sure he was going to put his foot in his mouth.

Luckily Darin made no answer. He was never big on conversation. Brad just let the silence surround them, gradually breaking them off into their own worlds.

He stayed awake for quite a while longer, wondering if Darin was also awake. Now that he had an explanation for this crazy week, Brad did not know what to do with it. He couldn't tell anyone, not even Lance. This was too ticklish. Sure, Lance was a good kid. But would you trust him with your life? Not really. If Darin ever found out that Brad told someone his secret—well, that might be a matter of life and death. But what to do about the girls? Tanya was plotting something terrible by the sounds of it. Brad did not want this stupid war to go any further. Sure, Darin had done a lot of dumb stuff. But the guy's life was miserable enough. The last thing he needed was to get singled out and humiliated by the girls. Besides that, it wasn't safe. Darin was a desperate guy with good reason to be desperate. Even if you didn't feel sorry for him, you didn't want to mess with people like that.

Brad decided that he would talk to Tanya about it tomorrow. *If* he could manage to talk with her alone. With Courtney on the prowl that would not be easy.

The Ultimate Weapon

As she entered the plastic kitchen for supper the next evening, Tanya felt a tap on her shoulder. It was Lance. His right eye was swollen shut—so puffed up and purple that she almost imagined she could see it throbbing.

"Yuk, what happened to you?" Tanya said.

"Our counselor beats us," Lance said with a straight face. Then, barely moving his mouth, he said, "I've got a message for you from Brad. Don't let Courtney see."

Tanya stared at him with distrust. Now what? Ordinarily she would not have had anything to do with anyone who tried to exclude Courtney. But Courtney had gone beyond disgusting, in Tanya's view. If Tanya heard anymore from her about what a wonderful person Brad was she would scream. She glanced around to see where Courtney was. As usual Courtney was distracted, sneaking coy looks at Brad Walker. Lance pressed a wad of paper in her hand and casually walked away. With her back to Courtney, Tanya read the note:

Need to talk to you alone.
Minus your friend.
As soon as possible.
Get away from her and I'll find you.

The note was unsigned. That made Tanya nervous. Whatever Brad was up to, he wanted it kept secret. He was making sure he left no evidence.

All through supper Tanya debated about whether to do what Brad wanted. Anything that involved Meadow Village had been bad news all week. Why should this be any different? She even thought about showing the note to Courtney. It would serve Brad right for sneaking around. Besides, Courtney would throw a huge fit. That would be the end of all this oohing and aahing about the wonderful Brad Walker.

But then Tanya was totally stumped in her sworn quest for revenge on Darin. She quickly dismissed whatever plan she came up with as too risky, too stupid, or just plain wrong. The war between the villages had drawn so much attention that neither side had much chance of getting away with anything. Yet she had to come up with something. Allison and some of the others were pestering her about it all the time.

Again Tanya mulled over Brad's request. Probably he just wanted her to get Courtney out of his life. But maybe he knew something that could help her get Darin. After all, Brad had made it clear that he did not like Darin.

Slipping away from Courtney after supper was no problem for Tanya. Courtney hardly seemed to know she existed. Brad was the one who would have trouble giving her the slip. But that was his problem. Tanya strolled down the main wagon road back toward the camp entrance. She stopped by the horse barn to watch Wrangler Rick saddle up some of the horses for an evening ride. She leaned on the wooden fence, ignoring the heavy smell of manure that wafted over from the barn.

A few minutes later Brad jogged down the trail. He was streaming sweat and gulping for air when he arrived.

"Sweat and manure," Tanya commented. "This ought to clean out the sinuses."

Brad wrinkled his nose at the horses who were plodding past them as they left the corral. He wiped his forehead on his shirt. "I had to make kind of a long loop through the woods to make sure I wasn't followed," he said.

"Oh, is someone making a nuisance of herself?" Tanya asked innocently.

"That's a minor problem," said Brad. "We've got a bigger one." He checked the trail to make sure no one was coming. "Let's make this quick. It's about Darin. You're planning something for him, right? For getting even. Just you?"

"Maybe," said Tanya. She leaned her chin on the fence and looked out at the corral to avoid his eyes. How did he know? If this news was all over camp that made her situation hopeless. She would never get away with anything.

"I happen to know, so you don't have to pretend," Brad said, impatiently. "Look, this is more serious than you think. Don't do anything to Darin. Please, just leave him alone. Okay?"

"Why should I?" asked Tanya, icily. "He didn't leave us alone."

Out of the corner of her eye she saw Brad fidgeting like she had never seen him. Several times he started to speak and then thought better of it. Tanya did not make it any easier for him. She continued to face the other direction.

Finally Brad came to a decision. "Tanya, I'm going to tell you something really important. But you have to promise that you will never, never tell a soul or even hint that you have any clue of this."

"Maybe," Tanya said. She was curious now. She worked doubly hard to disguise the fact. But her faked indifference pushed him to the edge of his patience.

"Fine! Go ahead!" he said, bitterly. "Do what you're going to do! Just don't come crying to me when it's all over."

"All right," Tanya said. "I won't tell anyone. What's the big secret?"

"Promise?" Brad insisted.

"Promise."

Brad checked down the road one more time. "Darin has some big problems," he said in a hushed voice. "He's a bed wetter. All of those lies he's been telling? He's just been trying to keep it covered up."

Tanya stared hard at Brad. Was he pulling her leg? Come on, a bed wetter? At his age? "This better not be another one of your—"

"It isn't, believe me," Brad interrupted. "This isn't funny anymore. This isn't any little get-even stuff between the villages. This is sad. Darin is one messed-up kid, and he's desperate. I mean the guy's in such a panic that he burns his own sleeping bag and dumps it in the woods."

Tanya stared at him, stunned. If this was really true, then that kid had major problems all right. Not that it excused him. Not by a long shot. Darin could have gotten her in big trouble with that midnight swim story and that burned sleeping bag story. He didn't care one bit about her. He was still a creep.

"Does anyone else know about this?" she asked.

"Nobody," Brad said firmly. "Not a soul. I only found out last night. So will you call it off? You don't have to like the guy. But just leave him alone, will you?"

"Yeah, sure," Tanya said. She was still trying to sort through what to do and so she did not say it with any conviction. But it seemed good enough for Brad.

"Good," he said. He started to jog back toward the villages. "And tell Courtney I think she's nice but I don't want a girlfriend."

Tell her yourself, Tanya thought with a smile. She isn't going to take it from me.

She waited for several moments by the corral until the horses disappeared up the ridge trail. Then she slowly walked back down the wagon road, squinting into the low-hanging sun. No clear decision jumped out at her. Part of her was grateful that Brad had warned her away from a bad situation. All the more reason for her to follow her instincts and drop the whole matter.

But part of her wished Brad had kept his mouth shut. Try as she might to feel sorry for Darin, she still hated him. She was glad he had problems—he deserved them! Maybe that just showed there was some justice in the world after all. It certainly did not give him the right to do what he had done to her!

And now she had the ultimate weapon of revenge. She knew the secret that Darin was terrified of exposing. She knew his worst weakness. It solved the problem she had been struggling with all day. Now she could carry out her promise to totally humiliate that creep without any fear of being caught. All she had to do was open her mouth and Darin's name would be mud throughout the camp. Back home, too, for that matter. It was so easy.

The temptation of total victory over Darin Chatfield made her smile. She drew pleasure for a moment just imagining Darin's shame.

But something did not feel right. Almost as soon as she imagined it, the taste of victory began to sour in her mind. Brad was right, this *was* pretty serious stuff. The weapon was too powerful. Darin could end up with some really ugly scars from all this.

Besides, whenever she did something wrong there always turned out to be some hidden cost she had not planned on. Already she could see the outlines of some of those hidden costs. What about Brad? Courtney was right, in her gooey way. Brad was probably the nicest boy in the whole camp. He had trusted her completely. She could tell it hadn't been easy for him to do. Tanya had promised him she would not tell. If she broke that promise now it would be like stomping on his face. The more she thought about it, the more she realized that she couldn't betray Brad.

So now what? She had told Brad she wouldn't do anything to Darin, and there were good reasons to stick to that. But she had told the girls that she *would* do something. And she still had a score to settle with that creep. She kicked at some loose gravel on the road in frustration.

Tanya didn't want to ruin Darin's whole life. She just wanted to nick him to prove that she would stand up for herself. She needed a dart, and all she had was a sledgehammer. Unless . . .

She came to a stop in the road. Maybe she could use this bed-wetting stuff. But not full strength. Just a little bit. So little that Brad wouldn't have to know anything about it. Only Darin. And he wouldn't know what hit him or who hit him!

Tanya rubbed her hands in glee as she thought of a plan. She had been studying Darin ever since that first false rumor about the swim, looking for some way to get him. She had observed his habits, his routines.

Meadow Village was due to ride first thing in the morning—their last ride of the week. Tanya remembered seeing that on the schedule posted at the horse barn. Last time Darin had ridden that big black horse, Rebel. He probably thought the name was cool. Tanya had heard him say that Rebel was "his horse." Well, if he was going to ride Rebel in the morning, maybe there would be a message for him. Just a little one. Darin could destroy the evidence before anyone else saw it. He wouldn't know who wrote it. But boy, would it make him sweat!

Tanya returned to the corral to wait for the end of the trail ride. She was sure Wrangler Rick wouldn't mind a little extra help cleaning up the barn after the last ride.

TWELVE

Broken Bottle

I get Pharoah!" shouted Brad.

"I call Rebel!" yelled Darin.

"I get anybody but Lord Godiva," said Lance.

"Whoa! Hold on," said Wrangler Rick, grabbing the two lead boys with his long arms. "You ought to know the rules by now. You stay out until I let you in. I'm not having any fighting over the horses."

"Can I have Pharoah?" Brad asked in his most polite voice.

"That's better," said Rick. "Go on in. Next request?" Brad walked almost to the end of the stalls where the big chestnut horse named Pharoah was standing. "No offense Skeeter," he said as he passed the smaller animal.

Behind him he heard three of the others begging for a buckskin horse name Sheik. Brad knew it would take Wrangler Rick a few minutes to sort out which of the three had not yet ridden that popular buckskin. Meanwhile, Brad heard Darin ask for Rebel, the horse he had ridden on both previous rides.

Rebel and Pharoah stood side by side in a wide stall. Wrangler had been busy recently. The stalls were swept out and fresh hay had been brought in. Brad patted Pharoah on the flank. "You going to give me a good ride this morning, big guy?"

Since it was the first ride of the day, the horses had to be saddled and bridled. Brad pulled the saddle blanket over the horse and adjusted it carefully. Then he slung the saddle up and over. He pulled the cinch belt as tight as he could under the horse's belly. Pharoah tossed his head and turned to stare at Brad.

Brad studied the cinch. "You puffed your stomach out, didn't you?" he asked with a laugh. Wrangler had told them how some horses swelled up their bellies when the cinch was tightened to keep it from being really snug. "Sorry, I can't go riding you with a loose saddle." He pushed his knee into Pharoah's belly and pulled again on the belt, just as Wrangler had taught them.

The rest of Meadow Village came into the stalls. Apparently the argument over Sheik was settled. Darin already had the blanket on Rebel and was reaching for the saddle. Brad was constantly aware of Darin now. All he wanted was for the kid to get through the week with no more problems. He even prayed about that. He was glad that no one was fighting Darin for that favorite horse of his.

The bridles for Pharoah and Rebel were hung on hooks between the two horses. Now came the part that Brad did not like—putting the bit in the horse's mouth. Most horses cared even less for the bit than they did for a tight cinch. Brad hated trying to force it into the horse's clenched teeth. He did not want to push too hard and get the horse mad, especially with his hand so close to those huge teeth.

Brad plucked Pharoah's bridle off the hook and checked the label just to be sure. Yep, "Pharoah" was written in black magic marker across a strip of tape. As he was about to begin the unpleasant process of bridling, he noticed the label on the other bridle. Something was written in red pen above Rebel's name. Brad bent closer.

What he read gave his heart a jolt! In small but neat letters were the words "bed wetter." Brad gulped, his heart racing. Who had done that? Tanya? It had to be Tanya. What was she trying to do?

Brad had no time to think. He dared not imagine what would happen if Darin saw that. Desperately he lifted the bridle and turned his back to Darin. He tried to peel off the tape. But it was stuck on too well. He tried to scrape the words off. But his fingernails were not long enough. In a panic, he licked his thumb and tried to smear the words. But although the red ink bled a little into pink, the words stood out clearly.

"Hey, give me my bridle," Darin said. Before Brad could react, Darin grabbed the bridle.

Brad was frozen with a sick horror as he watched Darin approach Rebel. Maybe he'll miss it, Brad thought. Please! Please!

Suddenly Darin stopped dead in his tracks. A chill swept through Brad's body as Darin wheeled and glared at Brad. Brad had never seen such a look of murderous hatred before. He backed out of the stall." "I didn't put that there," he protested. "I just saw it and was trying to take it off!"

Darin took a menacing step toward him. His nostrils flared like a horse's, and if any horse had his teeth clenched as tightly as Darin's, there was no way a bit would ever pass through those lips. Darin quickly scanned the stall. His eyes lit upon an empty pop bottle that someone had left on the ground next to a post. He bent down to pick up the bottle. He lifted it above his shoulder and took two slow steps toward Brad. Then, his face twisted in anger, Darin charged.

Brad backpedaled toward the walled side of the horse barn. He ducked as the bottle came flashing at his head. The glass whisked past his ear and crashed into a post. Rebel reared up and let out a loud trembling whinny. Pharoah stamped and kicked and strained at his halter rope.

The bottle broke off at the bottom, leaving a jagged cyclinder of glass. Darin looked at it, hatred still burning in his eyes. Brad backed up against the rough wood of the wall. He was trapped. God, help me! This guy's nuts! he thought.

Brad was never convinced that Darin meant to use his lethal weapon. Neither was he totally sure he did not. But before Darin could make another move, Red Dog grabbed his wrists from behind. Darin started to thrash, but Red Dog was far too powerful. He kept squeezing Darin's wrist as he wrestled him to the ground. The bottle fell.

Red Dog lay on top of Darin, still holding his wrists. For a moment no one said anything. Red Dog just looked calmly into those eyes still brimming with rage. He kept Darin locked up so that he could not move a muscle. The other boys stood behind Red Dog, their eyes wide in fear and confusion.

When Darin finally stopped struggling, Red Dog looked up at Brad. His face was flushed and he was breathing hard but showed no other sign that anything particularly disturbed him. "Looks like a few of us need to have a little chat with the director," he said. "Rick, can you take the rest of my boys on the trail by yourself?"

Brad had never set foot in the camp office before. All that he knew about it was that the camp director, Wrangler Rick, and some of the kitchen help slept there. It seemed to be a small, old farmhouse.

Brad sat alone in one tiny room that was almost entirely filled by a desk cluttered with stacks of green camp forms. It smelled like a coffee factory, thanks to an automatic coffee maker perking away on top of a file cabinet in the corner. Brad sat nervously on a vinyl chair. He shivered even though the room was not cold.

He was waiting for Pat to finish talking to Darin in another room. Since there was no clock on the wall, Brad had no idea how long he had sat so far. Probably not as long as it seemed, he thought. He could not make up his mind if he wanted the time to pass or to just drag on into infinity. What could he tell Pat that anyone would believe? He had already tried the story on Red Dog. Although the counselor listened patiently it did not take a genius to see he was more than skeptical. Brad had to admit he wouldn't believe it either if he were Red Dog. Some unknown person secretly wrote out those words on a bridle that Brad happened to find. And Brad happened to know that the words were meant for Darin and tried to protect him. Right!

He had learned one lesson from this anyway. He would never trust anyone again as long as he lived. Tanya had seen to that. Boy, how stupid he had been to count on her!

Red Dog opened the door and ambled slowly to the coffee maker. He filled a mug and took a short sip. A droplet of coffee hung on his mustache.

"Pat will be in soon," Red Dog said. "Darin's on the phone right now. He's calling home. Looks like his week at camp is over."

Brad sighed. "I don't blame him. He's had a terrible week."

Red Dog snorted. "No, that's the sad thing. He was having one of the best weeks of his life. Yesterday he told me he didn't ever want to leave Camp Grubstake."

"Why would he say that?" Brad said, stunned.

Red Dog took a longer sip this time. Then he squeezed past Brad again to make sure the door was shut. "Because even with all the trouble he went through with the nighttime stuff, this was a picnic compared to an average week at home."

Brad had thought that Darin might have some serious problems. But finding out for sure hit him hard. Brad's own parents were loving. Sure, they had their arguments and battles, but they cared for him. What would it be like to have parents who were just plain mean? No wonder Darin was mean.

Brad looked out the window again and saw the sparse vegetation of the south-facing slope. It's not his fault, he thought. Darin's stuck on a south-facing slope. Tough for anything to grow there. Doesn't matter how strong the plant is. Conditions are just too harsh. Put him in a north-facing family, Darin might do alright. Probably wouldn't wet the bed, either.

"You know those poison-pen letters from the girls?" Brad asked. "I thought something was funny about that. No one else was fooled for a second. But it was like Darin really thought his letter was from home."

Red Dog arched an eyebrow and nodded. "You're probably right. I can't tell you much about him because it's not really your business to know. But, yeah, he's probably used to hearing the kind of words that were in those letters. His grandmother brought him to camp and she sort of hinted something wasn't right. Maybe Pat can contact some people and see if we can't get help for him. But shoot," he said, sadly. "It's too bad people couldn't let him alone so that he could stay."

Brad felt a lump in his throat. He knew this wasn't fair—for Darin or for him. "But I tried," he muttered, looking out the window at nothing. "No one believes me, but I tried."

"How long have you known about Darin's problem?" Red Dog asked.

"Found out the night before last."

"Anyone else know?"

Oh, yes. Tanya knew. This was all her doing. Or else she blabbed and someone else wrote those words. Either way it was her fault. Brad thought about bringing Tanya into this. That would bring more trouble. Tanya would deny it, and the all the fighting and backbiting would just start up all over again. Worse than before probably.

Brad was sick over thinking about Darin going back to that awful home. He was angry about almost having his head cut open. But to his disgust he couldn't even bring himself to mention Tanya. He was too tired, too upset with it all to go after her. He had lost all respect for Tanya, but he wasn't going to fight her. What was the use?

"One other person knows," he said simply.

"And you're not saying who?" Red Dog asked.

Brad shook his head.

Red Dog sighed heavily. "Son, I don't really think you're the kind of person who would try to hurt Darin this much. But I got to face facts. Just give me a remotely reasonable explanation and I'll buy it."

"What's the use?" Brad said, bitterly. "I can't prove anything. Just my luck. I try to protect Darin and I'm the one who gets in trouble. Wonderful stroke of luck, huh?"

"Well, you did have *some* luck," Red Dog said.

"Sure. What's that?"

"You're lucky you weren't hit with that bottle."

THIRTEEN

Tanya's Turn

Camp Grubstake may have been spread out over six hundred acres, but that did not prevent the news of Darin's attack from reaching every camper within an hour. Forest Village got a second-hand report from some kids in Far Village who were a little sketchy on the details. All they knew for sure was that Darin had gone after Brad in the barn with a bottle. They didn't think anyone was seriously hurt.

Courtney screamed and started crying when she heard Brad was involved. Her performance would have been funny, Tanya thought, if this were not so serious. Poke stuck her hands in her pocket and looked defeated. Tanya felt as though she had finally crawled out of a deep, ugly pit of slime only to fall right back in again. That little note on the bridle was supposed to have been the final curtain that brought the fighting to an end. The note was to have been seen by Darin only. He would have known what it meant. That would have put him in his place. Then he would have destroyed the words and no one else would ever know. She would have gotten justice, but in a quiet way that would remain secret forever.

Tanya felt so shaky she had to sit down at the picnic bench. What had gone wrong? Had someone else ridden Rebel? If so, how did they know the message was meant for Darin? Had Darin found it and suspected Brad for some reason? That thought collapsed the pit of her stomach. How could she have been so stupid? Of course Darin would suspect someone in his own village! Maybe he even suspected that Brad knew his secret. What a dope! Her dumb stunt could have landed Brad in the hospital.

And that was far from the worst of it. Her secret trick was no longer a secret. Brad knew full well that she was the only person who could have written that note. Now she was in really deep trouble with him.

Poke seemed terribly depressed by the report. "A bottle!" she said, wearily. "I don't get it. Sometimes I wonder why we bother running a Bible camp. I don't know if we're making a bit of difference to these kids."

Her words stung Tanya as badly as the news of the fight. It was all Tanya's fault that Poke was feeling so defeated. Poke *had* made a difference, at least in Tanya's week. Tanya had never met anyone she admired so much. Poke was so trusting and so caring she just made you feel warm all over.

Poke had shown the power of forgiveness the way God meant it to be. The dumb stunts that the villages had been pulling in their feud had shown what God's laws were supposed to prevent. No forgiveness, just revenge and hatred growing until everyone was miserable. Poke had done her job. She had shown them a way out when she had forgiven Tanya for her poison-pen routine. Tanya had let her down but Poke had not let it get in the way. She knew how to forgive. Why didn't Tanya?

It overwhelmed Tanya to think how many people she had let down. Brad, Poke, Darin, God, probably more. She wished a hundred times that she could take back that moment when she pulled out her red pen. But what was done was done.

"You're the best counselor there is, Poke," she said, trying to cheer her up.

Poke smiled weakly. She walked over to the table. Tanya hoped for and expected a big hug. But Poke only jabbed a finger in Tanya's stomach. "Thanks," she said, trying to summon a smile.

That was it. Tanya was not going to let her down. Or Brad or God or even Darin. The creep. For the first time it did not sound quite right attaching those two words to Darin's name. Even Darin had to be forgiven. Somehow.

Along the shaded wagon road she ran into Brad coming the other way. He walked slowly, stooping several times to scoop up stones to throw idly into the trees. With woods growing on both sides of the road there was no way to avoid him.

Brad did not even look at her.

"Brad, wait," she said, as he started to go by her.

Brad turned toward her. There was an emptiness in his eyes as if he was looking at someone who did not exist. "Are you okay?" Tanya asked awkwardly.

"I'll live," he said, coldly. He turned to go, as if that was as many words as he had to waste on her.

"Are you in any trouble?" she asked. Brad nodded. "Brad, I'm sorry. It was a stupid thing to do. I didn't think anyone would know. I just wanted to give Darin a little jab. I'm going to go tell Pat what happened. At least you won't be in any trouble."

"Suit yourself," said Brad with indifference.

"Why did he think it was you?" Tanya asked.

"I saw what you wrote," Brad said. "I tried to get it off. He thought I was putting it on."

Tanya felt so foolish she could not think of a thing to say.

Brad seemed caught in the spell of some serious thought. "I know you can't stand Darin," he said at last. "But did you ever try to imagine what it would be like to be him and go through a week like this?"

"No," Tanya admitted.

"I can't help imagining it. I can hardly get my mind on anything else," Brad said.

"Well," Tanya said, awkwardly. She blushed a little. "I guess it wouldn't be too neat."

"No kidding!" Brad said. "And last night he called this the best week of his life. This is as *good* as it gets for him. The rest is worse. That's what he's going back to now."

"Right now?" Tanya asked.

"As long as it takes his grandmother to come get him," Brad said.

That was too much for Tanya. She took off running down the road. She did not know exactly what she was going to do when she got there. All she knew for sure was that she had to reach Pat before the grandmother came.

She burst into the front door of the office, gulping air. There was Darin sitting sullenly in an old chair that badly needed reupholstering. Pat and Red Dog both stood in the hall with their arms crossed. Tanya saw no grandmother.

"Pat," she gushed. Being totally out of breath helped. Somehow the words spilled out more easily in gasps and spurts than if she had been standing clearing her throat.

"I'm the one . . . who wrote those words . . . on the bridle," she said. "It was dumb. But it was just me . . . not Brad."

"I see," said Pat, severely. "And how exactly did you come to write exactly what you wrote?"

Tanya looked at Darin. His eyes narrowed in resentment. She pictured a grandmother in a car on the road, nearing the camp.

"I'll explain it all," she said. "But I need to talk to Darin first. Alone. Can I?" She could hardly believe what she was saying.

Pat and Red Dog exchanged puzzled glances. Pat hesitated. Red Dog seemed to be searching the room. Tanya wondered if he were checking for weapons that Darin might use.

Finally Pat said, "We'll be right outside the door."

Not until they left did Tanya really begin to get nervous. Darin glared at her. Tanya tried to ignore it and think about what Brad had told her. "I'm sorry, Darin," she said quietly. "What I did was really dumb and mean. I wish I had never done it."

Her words had no effect on Darin.

"No one else knows," Tanya continued.

Darin snorted in disbelief.

"Honest," Tanya said. "Brad was the only one who knew. He only told me because he wanted to help you."

Darin snorted again. Tanya turned on him angrily. He really was such a creep. "It's true!" she snapped. "Brad knew that I was planning to do something to you." She almost started to say that Brad felt sorry for him, but stopped herself in time. That was the last thing Darin wanted to hear.

"He thought that I might discover your secret and go blabbing it," Tanya continued. She felt funny standing while he was sitting, so she plopped herself down next to him. Darin instinctively pulled away. "Or do something else equally mean," Tanya continued. "He only told me because nothing else would make me stop. He made me promise not to tell anyone."

Darin snorted again. "Right!" he scoffed.

"Can't you see what he was doing in the barn?" Tanya said, her voice rising in frustration. "I was the one who wrote the words. He saw it and tried to get it off. He's not your enemy! He's on your side."

At last she had said something that did not provoke a snort. Darin seemed to be following her logic this time. "Maybe it happened like you said," he said. "So what do you want from me?"

"I don't want anything," Tanya said. The more she talked, the braver she felt. In fact she had never felt so brave in her whole life. "But Brad does. He wants you to stay at camp. Those guys at Meadow Village all do. You saw how they backed you up when they thought I burned your sleeping bag. They don't want you to go."

Darin looked a little sheepish about the sleeping bag incident. "Right," he said, shifting uncomfortably in his chair. "After I just about slice him open, he wants me to stay."

"It was all a big mistake. That was my fault," Tanya said. "Brad knows that. He's madder at me than he is at you." Boy, was that the truth, she thought. Brad would never trust her again.

That seemed to catch Darin off balance. "Maybe I'll stay and maybe I won't," he said.

"None of the kids will ever know," Tanya said. "I promise. And it's no big deal to me anyway." She got up to leave. "Now are you going to stay?"

Darin snorted again.

"Would you quit snorting and give me an answer?" Tanya said, and she couldn't help but laugh. For an instant she worried that Darin would think she was laughing at him. But the corner of his mouth twitched just a little in the barest trace of a smile that instantly disappeared.

"Maybe I will and maybe I won't."

Impulsively Tanya handed him the phone. "Maybe your ride hasn't left yet," she said eagerly.

"Got anything else to say?" Darin said.

"Nope." Tanya headed for the door without looking back. But just before the screen door slammed, she heard the click of a phone being dialed.

Suddenly it occurred to her that Pat might have made Darin go home. "I didn't blow it again, did I?" she asked anxiously. "I mean, is it okay if Darin stays?"

Pat stared at her in total bewilderment. "Does he want to?" she asked. "He's on the phone now."

"Let me check this out," Pat said. As she opened the screen door she turned to Tanya. "You wait here, young lady. I've got a few things to say to you."

But Tanya was pretty sure the worst was over. The only problem left was convincing Brad she wasn't as awful as he thought. And she had already thought of a start. "I'll bet if I can help him get Courtney out of his hair, he'll be grateful for life."

Darin's grandmother did show up to take him home. But not until Saturday when all the campers left. The last thing Brad saw that day was Courtney exchanging addresses with a boy from Far Village. Thank you, Tanya, he thought. I don't know how you did it, and I don't want to know.

"How did your week go?" Brad's dad asked as he tossed a sleeping bag in the trunk of their car.

"You're not going to believe half of it."